Maigret's Anger

'Extraordinary masterpiec[...]

'A brilliant writer'   – India Knight

'Intense atmosphere and resonant detail . . . make Simenon's
fiction remarkably like life'   – Julian Barnes

'A truly wonderful writer . . . marvellously readable – lucid,
simple, absolutely in tune with the world he creates'
                                                        – Muriel Spark

'Few writers have ever conveyed with such a sure touch, the
bleakness of human life'   – A. N. Wilson

'Compelling, remorseless, brilliant'   – John Gray

'A writer of genius, one whose simplicity of language creates
indelible images that the florid stylists of our own day can
only dream of'   – *Daily Mail*

'The mysteries of the human personality are revealed in all
their disconcerting complexity'   – Anita Brookner

'One of the greatest writers of our time' – *The Sunday Times*

'I love reading Simenon. He makes me think of Chekhov'
                                                    – William Faulkner

'One of the great psychological novelists of this century'
                                                       – *Independent*

'The greatest of all, the most genuine novelist we have had
in literature'   – André Gide

'Simenon ought to be spoken of in the same breath as
Camus, Beckett and Kafka'   – *Independent on Sunday*

GEORGES SIMENON

Maigret's Anger

Translated by WILLIAM HOBSON

PENGUIN BOOKS

PENGUIN CLASSICS

UK | USA | Canada | Ireland | Australia
India | New Zealand | South Africa

Penguin Books is part of the Penguin Random House group of companies
whose addresses can be found at global.penguinrandomhouse.com.

First published in French as *La Colère de Maigret* (Presses de la Cité, 1963)
This translation first published 2018
002

Set in 12.5/15 pt Dante MT Std
Typeset by Jouve (UK), Milton Keynes
Printed and bound in Great Britain by Clays Ltd, Elcograf S.p.A.

ISBN: 978–0–241–30401–3

www.greenpenguin.co.uk

Maigret's Anger

1.

It was 12.15 when Maigret went through the permanently cool archway and out of the gate flanked by two uniformed policemen who were hugging the walls to get a little shade. He waved to them, then stood for a moment motionless and undecided, looking towards the courtyard, then towards Place Dauphine, then back towards the courtyard.

Under the pretence of relighting his pipe he had stopped several times in the corridor upstairs, then on the dusty stairs, in the hope that one of his colleagues or inspectors would suddenly appear from somewhere. It was unusual for the stairs to be deserted at that time, but this year on 12 June a holiday atmosphere already prevailed at police headquarters.

Some people had gone away at the start of the month to avoid the crush of July and August, while others were getting ready for the annual exodus. After a dismal spring, it had suddenly turned hot that morning, and Maigret had worked in his shirt-sleeves with the windows open.

Apart from the daily briefing with the head of the Police Judiciaire and one or two visits to the inspectors' office, he had spent the morning on his own, working on a tedious administrative chore he had started a few days earlier. Files piled up in front of him, and every now and then he would lift his head like a schoolboy, eyes fixed on the leaves hanging motionless on the trees, listening to Paris's murmur, which had just taken on the particular quality it has on hot summer days.

For the past fortnight he hadn't missed a single meal at Boulevard Richard-Lenoir or been disturbed in the evening or at night.

Normally he would have turned left on the embankment and headed towards Pont Saint-Michel to get a bus or taxi. The courtyard remained resolutely empty. No one came and joined him.

Eventually, with a slight shrug of his shoulders, he turned right instead, and on reaching Place Dauphine cut across the square. Leaving his office, he had suddenly felt like going to the Brasserie Dauphine for an aperitif, despite the advice of his friend Pardon, the doctor in Rue Picpus, at whose house he and Madame Maigret had had dinner the previous week.

He had been good for several weeks, restricting himself to a glass of wine at meals and the occasional beer with his wife when they went out in the evening.

Now suddenly he missed the smell of the bistro on Place Dauphine, the aniseed taste of its aperitifs that went down so well on days like this. He had been hoping to run into someone who would drag him off there, but no such luck, and he felt guilty as he climbed the little brasserie's three steps. A long, low, red car was parked outside, which he looked at curiously.

Oh well! Pardon had advised him to take care of his liver but he hadn't barred him from having an aperitif – just one – after weeks of near total abstinence.

He recognized some familiar faces around the bar, at least a dozen members of the Police Judiciaire who had almost as little work as him and had left early. It happened from time to time: a few days' lull, the office quiet as the grave, just routine matters, as they were known, and then suddenly cases would flood in so fast that no one could catch their breath.

The men waved to him in greeting, squeezed up to make room for him at the bar. Pointing to the glasses filled with a milky-coloured drink, he muttered:

'Same here . . .'

The owner had already been there thirty years earlier, when Maigret had started at Quai des Orfèvres, but in those days he had been the son and heir. Now there was another son, wearing a white chef's hat in the kitchen, looking just as he had when he was a boy.

'How's things, chief?'

'Fine.'

The smell hadn't changed. Every little brasserie in Paris has its distinctive aroma. In this one, for instance, against a background of aperitifs and liqueurs, a connoisseur would have discerned the slightly sharp bouquet of the ordinary wines of the Loire and a preference for tarragon and chives in the cooking.

Maigret automatically read the menu on the slate: baby whiting from Brittany and veal liver *en papillottes*. As he did so, he caught sight of Lucas in the dining room with its paper tablecloths. No one was eating lunch yet, and Lucas seemed to have taken refuge in there to have a quiet chat with a man Maigret didn't recognize.

Lucas saw Maigret too. He hesitated, then got up and came out.

'Do you have a moment, chief? I think this might interest you . . .'

Maigret followed him, glass in hand. The stranger stood up. Lucas made the introductions: 'Antonio Farano . . . Do you know him?'

The name didn't ring any bells, but Maigret thought he had seen the handsome Italian with the movie star looks before. He was probably the owner of the red sports car outside. It went with his appearance, the flashy cut of his light-coloured clothes, the heavy signet ring he was wearing on his finger.

As the three men sat down, Lucas went on, 'He showed up at the office wanting to see me just after I'd left. Lapointe told him he might find me here . . .'

Maigret noticed that Lucas was also having an aperitif, while Farano was making do with a fruit juice.

'He's Émile Boulay's brother-in-law. He runs one of his clubs, the Paris-Strip on Rue de Berri . . .'

Lucas winked discreetly at his boss.

'Say what you just told me, Farano . . .'

'Well, my brother-in-law has disappeared . . .'

He still had his native accent.

'When?' asked Lucas.

'Last night, probably. We don't know exactly . . .'

He was overawed by Maigret. To distract from his nervousness, he took a cigarette case out of his pocket.

'Do you mind?'

'Go ahead . . .'

For Maigret's benefit, Lucas explained:

'You know Boulay, chief. He's the little guy who turned up from Le Havre four or five years ago . . .'

'Seven,' the Italian corrected him.

'Seven years ago, right . . . He bought his first club on Rue Pigalle, the Lotus, and now he's got four . . .'

Maigret wondered why Lucas wanted to involve him. He hardly ever had dealings with that world now he had taken over the Crime Squad. He used to know it well but he'd lost touch with it a little recently. He hadn't set foot in a club for at least two years, and he only knew a few of Pigalle's villains these days, mainly from the older generation, because it was a small world which was constantly changing.

'I wonder,' Lucas went on, 'if this hasn't got something to do with the Mazotti case . . .'

Ah, right! He was beginning to understand. Mazotti had been shot as he was leaving a bar on Rue Fontaine around three o'clock in the morning. When was that? About a month ago now, mid-May roughly. Maigret remembered a report from the ninth arrondissement, which he had passed on to Lucas, saying, 'Probably a settling of old scores . . . Do your best.'

Mazotti wasn't an Italian, like Farano, but a Corsican who had started out on the Côte d'Azur before coming up to Paris with a little gang he had put together.

'My brother-in-law didn't kill Mazotti,' Farano insisted with feeling. 'You know he's not that kind of person, Monsieur Lucas. Besides, you questioned him twice in your office.'

'I never accused him of killing Mazotti. He was just one of the people I called in because Mazotti had gone after them. Quite a crowd, in other words . . .'

Turning to Maigret, he explained:

'I'd actually called him in for questioning at eleven this morning, so I was surprised not to see him.'

'Doesn't he ever spend the night elsewhere?' Maigret asked ingenuously.

'Never. You obviously don't know him. That's just not his way. He loves my sister, family life. He'd never come home later than four in the morning.'

'And last night he didn't come home at all, is that it?'

'Yes, that's it.'

'Where were you?'

'At the Paris-Strip . . . We didn't shut until at least five. It's high season for us because Paris is already swarming with tourists. When I was cashing up, Marina rang to ask if I'd seen Émile – Marina's my sister. I hadn't seen my brother-in-law all night. He hardly ever came down to the Champs-Elysées.'

'Where are his other clubs?'

'They're all in Montmartre, a few hundred metres from each other. It was his idea to do it like that, and it worked out well. When you have clubs virtually next door to each other, you can shuffle performers around between them and keep overheads down.

'The Lotus is right at the top of Rue Pigalle, the Train Bleu's just around the corner in Rue Victor-Massé, and the Saint-Trop' is down the hill a bit, on Rue Notre-Dame-de-Lorette.

'Émile was unsure about opening a club in another part of town, and it was really the only one he didn't take care of himself. He let me run it for him.'

'So your sister rang you a little after five o'clock.'

'Yes. She's so used to being woken up by her husband.'

'What did you do?'

'I called the Lotus first, where they said he'd left at around eleven in the evening. He also went by the Train Bleu, but the cashier couldn't say exactly when . . . And the Saint-Trop' was closed when I tried to call.'

'Your brother wasn't meeting anyone last night as far as you know, was he?'

'No. I told you: he was a quiet man, very much a creature of habit. He'd have dinner at home—'

'What's his address?'

'Rue Victor-Massé—'

'In the same building as the Train Bleu?'

'No, three doors along . . . So, he'd have dinner, then he'd go to the Lotus first to supervise preparations for the night. That's the biggest club, and he ran it personally. Then he'd go down to the Saint-Trop' and stay there for a while, then he'd carry on to the Train Bleu, and then he'd start the whole circuit again . . . He did it two or three times a night because he liked to keep an eye on everything.'

'Was he in a dinner jacket?'

'No. He used to wear a dark suit, midnight blue, but never a dinner jacket. He wasn't that fussed about dressing stylishly.'

'You talk about him in the past.'

'Because I'm sure something's happened to him.'

Various tables were starting to eat, and Maigret found himself eyeing their plates of food and carafes of white wine. His glass was empty, but he resisted the urge to order another.

'Then what did you do?'

'I asked my sister to call me if there was any news, then went to bed.'

'Did she?'

'Around eight in the morning.'

'Where do you live?'

'Rue de Ponthieu.'

'Are you married?'

'Yes. My wife's Italian too. I spent the morning calling round the staff of the three clubs. I was trying to find out where he'd been seen last, and when. It's not easy . . . The clubs are packed most of the night, and everyone's concentrating on their work. Émile didn't stand out that much, either. He was a short, skinny guy whom customers never realized was the owner, and sometimes he'd stand out front with the doorman for hours.'

Lucas nodded in agreement.

'No one seems to have seen him after eleven thirty.'

'Who saw him last?'

'I haven't been able to ask everybody. Some of the barmen and musicians don't have telephones and I don't know most of the girls' addresses. I'll only be able to ask around properly this evening when everyone's at work.

'So far, the last person to have talked to him is the

Lotus' doorman, Louis Boubée, a tiny character no taller or heavier than a jockey, who's known around Montmartre as Mickey.

'Which means that, between eleven and eleven thirty, Émile came out of the Lotus and kept Mickey company on the pavement while he did his usual thing of rushing forward to open the door every time a car stopped.'

'Did they talk?'

'Émile wasn't much of a talker. Apparently he looked at his watch a few times before heading off down the street. Mickey thought he was going to the Saint-Trop'.'

'Did your brother-in-law have a car?'

'No. Not since the accident.'

'What accident?'

'It was seven years ago. He was still living in Le Havre, where he had a little club, the Monaco. One day he was driving to Rouen with his wife . . .'

'Was he already married to your sister?'

'This was his first wife, a Frenchwoman from around Le Havre called Marie Pirouet. She was expecting a child. In fact they were going to Rouen to consult a specialist. It was raining. As they were taking a corner, the car skidded and smashed into a tree. Émile's wife was killed instantly . . .'

'What about him?'

'He got off with just a gash to the cheek that left him with a scar. Most people in Montmartre think he was stabbed.'

'Did he love his wife?'

'Very much. He'd known her since he was a child . . .'

'Was he born in Le Havre?'

'In a village near it; I don't know which one. She was born there too. After her death he never touched a steering wheel again and wouldn't even get in a car if he could help it. He hardly ever took taxis in Paris, for instance. He walked a lot and when he had to he took the Métro. He didn't like leaving the ninth anyway.'

'Do you reckon someone's done away with him?'

'I think that if nothing had happened to him he would have been home a long time ago.'

'Did he live alone with your sister?'

'No. My mother lives with them, as does my other sister, Ada, who's his secretary. And then there's the two children: Émile and Marina have two children, you see. A three-year old boy, Lucien, and a little girl who's ten months old.'

'Do you suspect anyone?'

Antonio shook his head.

'Do you feel your brother-in-law's disappearance has anything to do with the Mazotti case?'

'One thing I'm sure of is that Émile didn't kill Mazotti.'

Maigret turned to Lucas, who had been in charge of the investigation.

'What about you?'

'I'm certain of that too, chief. I questioned him twice and he seemed to give me straight answers both times. As Antonio says, he's on the puny side, shy, almost – not the sort of character you'd expect to find running a string of nightclubs. Which is not to say that when it came to Mazotti, he couldn't look after himself.'

'How?'

'Mazotti and his gang had organized an extortion racket that wasn't original in the slightest but they'd got it down to a tee. They made out they were offering protection, but it was just a way of extorting money. They demanded different amounts each week from all the club owners . . .

'Most refused at first. There then followed a well-rehearsed routine. When the club was full Mazotti would come in with a couple of heavies. They'd sit at a table or the bar, whichever was free, order champagne and then pick a fight in the middle of an act. There'd be muttering first, then they'd start shouting, going after the barman or maître d', calling him a thief. Glasses would be smashed and it would end up in a free-for-all, more or less. Naturally most of the customers would leave, swearing never to come back. Next time Mazotti visited the owners preferred to pay up.'

'But Émile didn't?'

'No. He didn't send for the heavies either, like some of his colleagues. Not that it worked anyway, because Mazotti always bought them off in the end. His idea was to call in some dockers from Le Havre who were given the job of bringing Mazotti and his men into line . . .'

'When was the last set-to?'

'The night Mazotti died. He had gone to the Lotus around one in the morning with two of his regular sidekicks. Émile Boulay's dockers threw them out. It turned violent.'

'Was Émile there?'

'He hid behind the bar because he can't stand fighting . . . Afterwards Mazotti went to lick his wounds in a bar on

Rue Fontaine, Chez Jo, which was sort of his headquarters. There were four or five of them drinking at the back. When they came out at three in the morning a car drove past, and Mazotti was shot five times while one of his men took a bullet in the shoulder. We haven't found the car. No one's talked. I've questioned most of the club owners . . . I'm still investigating.'

'Where was Boulay at the time of the shooting?'

'It's not easy establishing facts in that world, as you know, chief . . . . Apparently he was in the Train Bleu, but I don't trust the witness statements that much.'

'Émile didn't kill Mazotti,' the Italian repeated.

'Did he carry a gun?'

'An automatic, yes. He had a police permit. That wasn't the gun Mazotti was killed with.'

Maigret sighed, then signalled to the waitress to fill their glasses as he had been dying to do for a while.

'I wanted to bring you up to date, chief,' Lucas explained, 'and I thought you'd be interested in hearing what Antonio had to say.'

'Everything I said was true.'

'I'd called Émile in for questioning this morning,' Lucas went on. 'I admit it bothers me that he then went missing last night.'

'What did you want to ask him?'

'It was just routine. I was going to ask him the same questions one last time, to check his answers against those he gave me the first time round and the other witness statements.'

'Did he seem scared either of the times he was in your office?'

'No. Annoyed, more like . . . He couldn't stand the thought of his name being in the papers. He kept saying that it would cause his business tremendous harm, that his clubs were quiet places, nothing ever went on in them, and that if he was associated with a settling of underworld scores, he'd never live it down.'

'That's true,' Antonio agreed, making as if to stand up. 'Do you need anything else from me? I should be getting back to my sisters and my mother. They're in a terrible state . . .'

Moments later they heard the roar of the red car as it sped off in the direction of Pont-Neuf. Maigret slowly took a sip of his aperitif, glanced sidelong at Lucas and sighed:

'Are you expected somewhere?'

'No. I was planning to . . .'

'Eat here?'

He nodded, making up Maigret's mind for him.

'In that case we'll eat together. I'll give my wife a call. You can order.'

'Are you going to have the mackerel?'

'And the veal liver *en papillotes*.'

The veal liver particularly caught his fancy, as well as the atmosphere of the bistro, which he hadn't been into for weeks.

The case wasn't particularly important, and Lucas hadn't needed any help on it before this. No one outside the underworld cared about Mazotti's death. Everyone knew that such score-settlings always ended up resolving themselves, even if just by more of the same.

The advantage to these cases was that the prosecutor's

office and examining magistrates didn't hound the police. As one magistrate used to say:

'That's one less prison bill to pay . . .'

The two men had lunch and chatted. Maigret learned some more about Émile Boulay and ended up becoming interested in this strange little man.

The son of a Norman fisherman, Émile had got a job as a waiter with the Compagnie Générale Transatlantique – 'Transat' for short – when he turned sixteen. This had been before the war. He sailed on the *Normandie* and found himself in New York when the fighting started in France.

It was hard to fathom how such a puny little man had been admitted into the American marines. Nonetheless, he had fought the whole war in that branch of the forces before taking up a job on the *Ile-de-France*, this time as a head waiter.

'You know, chief, almost all of them dream of going into business for themselves one day. Two years after he got married, Boulay bought a bar in Le Havre and wasted no time turning it into a dance club. Striptease was just starting to become popular in those days, and he seems to have immediately made a pretty serious pile.

'By the time of the accident and his wife's death, he was already planning to expand to Paris.'

'Did he keep the club in Le Havre?'

'He appointed a manager. One of his old shipmates from the *Ile-de-France* runs it for him. In Paris he bought the Lotus, which wasn't as successful then as it is now. It was a bit of a dive, a tourist trap like all the others round Place Pigalle.'

'Where did he meet Antonio's sister?'

'At the Lotus. She was working in the cloakroom. She was only eighteen.'

'What was Antonio doing in those days?'

'Working at the Renault factory in the body shop. He had come to France first, then sent for his mother and two sisters. They lived in Javel.'

'So Émile basically seems to have married the whole family . . . Have you been to his place?'

'No. I had a look around the Lotus and his other clubs but I didn't think I needed to go to his apartment.'

'Are you convinced he didn't kill Mazotti?'

'Why would he have? He was winning.'

'He might have been afraid.'

'No one in Montmartre thinks he did it.'

They had coffee in silence, and Maigret refused the calvados the owner offered him in his usual way. He had started with a couple of aperitifs but then only drunk a glass of Pouilly so felt pretty pleased with himself as he headed back to the Police Judiciaire with Lucas.

In his office he took off his jacket, loosened his tie and set about the administrative files. Nothing less than a complete reorganization of the police services was on the agenda, and he was expected to produce a report. He applied himself like a good student.

At times during the afternoon he found himself think-ing about Émile Boulay and the little Montmartre empire the former Transat employee had built up, about the young Italian with the red sports car and the apartment on Rue Victor-Massé where the three women lived with the children.

Meanwhile Lucas rang round the hospitals, the police stations. He circulated Boulay's description as well, but by six thirty nothing had come of his inquiries.

It was almost as hot that evening as it had been during the day. Maigret went for a walk with his wife and sat outside a café in Place de la République, nursing a glass of beer for almost an hour.

They talked mainly about their holidays. Many of the men passing by had their jackets over their arms; most of the women were wearing cotton print dresses.

The next day was a Thursday. Another glorious day. The daily reports made no mention of Émile Boulay; Lucas had no news either.

There was a violent but short-lived thunderstorm around eleven, after which steam seemed to be rising from the cobblestones. He went home for lunch, then returned to the office and the stack of files.

When it was time to leave Quai des Orfèvres there was still no news of the little man from Le Havre, and Lucas had spent a fruitless afternoon in Montmartre.

'Boubée, or Mickey, as he's known, who's been a doorman at the Lotus for years, does seem to be the last person to have seen him alive, chief. He thinks he remembers Émile turning the corner of Rue Pigalle and Rue Notre-Dame-de-Lorette as if he was going to the Saint-Trop', but he didn't really take any notice . . . I'll go back to Montmartre this evening when they'll all be at work.'

Lucas drew another blank on Thursday evening. At nine o'clock the following morning Maigret paused as he was going through the last of the daily reports, then called him into his office.

'He's been found,' he said, relighting his pipe.

'Alive?'

'Dead.'

'In Montmartre? In the Seine?'

Maigret handed him a report from the twentieth arrondissement. It stated that a man's dead body had been found at daybreak in Rue des Rondeaux, next to Père-Lachaise. The man was lying across the pavement, not far from the railway cutting. He was dressed in a dark blue suit, and his wallet contained a sum of money and an identity card in the name of Émile Boulay.

Lucas looked up, frowning.

'I wonder . . .' he began.

'Go on reading.'

The inspector was even more surprised by what followed. The report specified that the body, which had been taken to the Forensic Institute, was in an advanced state of decomposition.

It was true that Rue des Rondeaux was a cul-de-sac and not very busy, but still, a body couldn't have lain on the pavement there for two days, or even two hours, without being discovered.

'What do you reckon?'

'It's strange . . .'

'Have you read the whole thing?'

'Not the end.'

Émile Boulay had disappeared on Tuesday night. Given

the state of the body, it was likely that he had been killed that same night.

Two full days had elapsed since then, two swelteringly hot days.

It was hard to think why the murderer, or murderers, would have kept hold of the body all that time.

'That's even stranger!' Lucas exclaimed, putting the report on the desk.

The strangest thing of all was the fact that, according to initial findings, the murder hadn't been committed with a gun or a knife.

As far as could be discerned pending the autopsy, Émile Boulay had been strangled.

Despite their many years on the force, neither Maigret nor Lucas could remember a single underworld strangling.

Every neighbourhood of Paris, every social class, has its way of killing, so to speak, as it does its preferred method of committing suicide. There are streets where people throw themselves out of the window, others where they put their heads in charcoal or gas ovens, others where they take barbiturates.

Police similarly know the knifing neighbourhoods, the ones where coshes are used, the ones like Montmartre, say, where firearms predominate.

Not only had the little nightclub owner been strangled, but his murderer had then waited two days and three nights before disposing of his body.

Maigret was already opening the cupboard to get his jacket and hat.

'Let's go!' he muttered.

At last he had an excuse to put aside his administrative chore for a moment.

On a beautiful June morning, cooled by a light breeze, the two men headed off to the Forensic Institute.

2.

The pink buildings of the Forensic Institute on Quai de la Rapée look more like a pharmaceuticals laboratory, say, than the old morgue under the great clock of the Palais de Justice.

Behind a window in a bright office, Maigret and Lucas found an employee who recognized them immediately and said with an eager smile, 'This is about the fellow from Rue des Rondeaux, I assume?'

The electric clock above his head showed 10.05. Through the window they could see the barges on the other side of the Seine, moored off the warehouse docks of the Magasins Généraux.

'There's someone already waiting,' the official continued chattily. 'A relative apparently.'

'Did he give his name?'

'I'll ask him for that when he's identified the body and is ready to sign his statement.'

The man thought of the corpses in purely theoretical terms, as entries on filing cards.

'Where is he?'

'In the waiting room. You'll have to bide your time too, Monsieur Maigret. Doctor Morel is in the middle of his work.'

The corridor had white walls and light-coloured tiles.

The waiting room was equally bright, with its two benches and varnished wooden chairs, its large table that was only lacking a stack of magazines to complete the impression that you were at the dentist. The glossy walls were bare. Maigret had often wondered what sort of paintings or prints they could have put on them.

Antonio was sitting in one of the chairs, chin in hands. He was still a handsome young man, but his face was a bit puffy, as if he hadn't had enough sleep, his cheeks unshaven.

He stood up when the policemen came in.

'Have you seen him?' he asked.

'Not yet.'

'Nor have I. I've been waiting for over half an hour. That was definitely Émile's identity card they showed me though.'

'Who did?'

'An inspector with an odd name . . . Hang on . . . Mornique? Bornique?'

'Bornique, yes . . .'

Maigret and Lucas exchanged a look. Bornique from the twentieth arrondissement. They might have guessed. There were a few of his sort in local stations – not only inspectors but chief inspectors – who were the Police Judiciaire's sworn rivals and made it a point of honour to arrive at crime scenes before them.

Maigret had only learned that the body had been found from the daily reports, and the officers of the twentieth had been anything but idle since their discovery. Avoiding these excesses of zeal was precisely why he had been working for the past few weeks on a reorganization of the force.

'Do you think the doc's going to be much longer? The women are frantic.'

'Did Bornique go and tell them?'

'This morning. It wasn't even eight o'clock. They'd just got up and were seeing to the kids.

'"Which of you is Marina Boulay?" he asked.

'Then he handed my sister an identity card.

'"This is your husband's, is it? Do you recognize his photograph? When did you last see him?"

'You can imagine the scene. Ada immediately rang me at home. I was asleep. I didn't stop to have breakfast or make a cup of coffee. A few minutes later, I was in Rue Victor-Massé being treated as a suspect by the inspector, more or less.

'"Hey, who are you?"

'"The brother-in-law."

'"Of this lady?"

'"No. Of her husband."'

Antonio was very tense.

'I had a huge argument about my identifying the body rather than my sister. She insisted on coming. I didn't think it would be a pretty sight so I made her stay at home.'

He nervously lit a cigarette.

'Didn't the inspector come with you?'

'No. Apparently he's got something else to do. He told me that the clerk here would give me a form to fill out and sign.'

After a pause he added:

'You see, I was right to be worried. A couple of days

ago you didn't seem to believe me. Where is Rue des Rondeaux?'

'Beside Père-Lachaise cemetery.'

'I don't know it around there. What's it like?'

A door opened. Doctor Morel, who was wearing a white coat and cap, with a surgical mask under his chin, looked round for Maigret.

'I was told you were waiting for me, Maigret. Would you follow me?'

He showed them into a room where the only light came through frosted glass panes. The walls were lined with metal cabinets of the sort you find in government offices, except that they were of an unusual size. A body covered with a sheet lay on a gurney.

'Best if his brother-in-law identifies him first,' said Maigret.

The sheet was pulled back from the face in the customary way. The dead man had almost a centimetre's growth of beard, which was reddish in colour, like his hair. His skin was a shade of blue and the scar on his left cheek that Antonio had talked about at the Brasserie Dauphine was clearly visible.

Under the sheet his body looked slight and thin.

'Is that definitely him?'

'Of course it is.'

Sensing the Italian felt nauseous, Maigret sent him to the office with Lucas to complete the paperwork.

'Shall we put him away?' asked the doctor, signalling to a man in a grey coat who had already opened one of the drawers. 'Will you come with me, Maigret?'

He took him into an office with a wash-basin and, as he talked, disinfected his hands and face, took off his white coat and looked like an ordinary man again.

'I imagine you'd like some preliminary findings before you get my report? As usual we'll have to do some analyses which will take several days. What I can tell now is that the body shows no sign of wounds. The man was strangled, or, more precisely . . .'

Morel searched for the right word, as if he wasn't too sure of himself.

'This isn't official, right? I shan't be so categorical in my report . . . If I had to piece together the murder on the basis of the post-mortem, I'd say that the victim was attacked from behind, that someone put their arm round his neck and pulled back so violently that a cervical vertebra snapped. The effect is similar to what you'd call whiplash.'

'So he was standing up, was he?'

'Yes, or possibly seated. I'm inclined to think that he was standing up and that he wasn't expecting to be attacked. There was no real struggle. He didn't put up any sort of fight. I carefully examined his nails and didn't find any strands of wool, which would indicate that he had grabbed hold of the attacker's clothes, or blood, or hair. There are no scratches on his hands either. Who is he?'

'A nightclub owner. Do you have any idea of the date of his death?'

'It's been at least two full days, three at the most, since the man died. Again off the record, I can't vouch for this, but I'd be inclined to add that, in my opinion, the body wasn't out in the open during that time. You'll have an initial report this evening.'

Lucas appeared.

'He's signed the papers . . . What shall I do with him? Send him back to Rue Victor-Massé?'

Maigret nodded because he still had to examine Émile's clothes and the contents of his pockets. This would be repeated more scientifically later in the laboratory.

The belongings were in another room, in a pile on a table. The dark-blue suit wasn't torn and there was only a little dust on it. No blood. It was barely crumpled. The black shoes were as clean as those of a man just stepping out of his house, with only two fresh scuffs in the leather.

Maigret would have put money on the murder being committed indoors rather than in the street, and on the body only being left on the pavement in Rue des Rondeaux late the previous night.

Where had it been brought from? A car had almost certainly been used. It hadn't been dragged along the pavement.

The contents of the pockets were something of a disappointment. Had Émile Boulay smoked? Apparently not. No pipe, no cigarettes, no lighter, no matches. None of those strands of tobacco you always find at the bottom of smokers' pockets.

A gold watch. Five hundred new franc notes and three fifties in the wallet. A few ten-franc notes loose in one of the pockets and some small change in another.

A bunch of keys, a penknife, a couple of handkerchiefs, one crumpled, the other neatly folded in his breast pocket. A small packet of aspirin and some peppermints.

Lucas, who was emptying the wallet, exclaimed:

'Look, my summons.'

A summons Émile Boulay would have been hard put to answer.

'I thought he carried an automatic,' muttered Maigret.

A gun wasn't among the objects spread out on the table, but there was a chequebook which Maigret leafed through. It was almost new. Only three cheque stubs. The only significant one was for 500,000 new francs made out 'to myself.'

It was dated 22 May.

'See that!' Lucas noticed immediately. 'That's when I called him in to Quai des Orfèvres for the second time. I had seen him first on 18 May, the day after Mazotti died.'

'Will you tell the laboratory to come and get all this and analyse it?'

A few minutes later the two men set off in the black car. Lucas drove slowly and deliberately.

'Where are we going, chief?'

'Rue des Rondeaux first. I want to see where he was found.'

Despite the cemetery and the railway track, the place didn't look sinister in the sunshine. As they drove up, they could see a knot of bystanders being marshalled by a couple of policemen, a few housewives looking out of their windows, some children playing. When the car stopped,

Maigret was greeted by Inspector Bornique, who declared with a studied air of modesty:

'I've been expecting you, sir. I thought you'd be coming and I made a point of . . .'

The policemen stepped aside, revealing the silhouette of a body drawn in chalk on the greyish pavement.

'Who found him?'

'A gas worker who starts his shift at five in the morning and lives in this building. That's his wife you can see at the window on the third floor. I've got his statement, of course. I was on night duty, as it happened . . .'

With the bystanders looking on, now wasn't the moment to take him to task.

'Tell me, Bornique, do you get the impression the body was pushed out of a car or left on the pavement?'

'Left, definitely.'

'On his back?'

'On his stomach. At first sight, you might have thought he was a drinker sleeping off a heavy night. Except for the smell . . . Oh goodness, that smell, I can't tell you . . .'

'I imagine you've questioned the neighbours?'

'All the ones who are at home. Women and old men, mainly, because the rest have gone out to work.'

'No one saw anything, heard anything?'

'Except for an old woman up on the fifth floor who apparently suffers from insomnia. It's true that the concierge thinks she doesn't really know what she's saying any more. She claims that around three thirty in the morning she heard a car braking. Not many come this far down the street as it's a dead end.'

'Did she hear voices?'

'No. Just a car door opening, then footsteps, then the door shutting again.'

'Did she look out of the window?'

'She's practically bedridden. At first she thought that someone in the building was ill and that they'd called an ambulance. She was expecting to hear the door open and shut again, but, after turning round, the car drove off almost immediately.'

With the air of a seasoned professional, Inspector Bornique added:

'I'll drop by at midday and this evening, when the menfolk will be home from work.'

'Have the men from the prosecutor's office been here?'

'Very early. They were done in no time. It was just a formality.'

Under the watchful eyes of the crowd, Maigret and Lucas got back into their car.

'Rue Victor-Massé.'

They drove past fruit and vegetable stalls piled high with cherries and peaches, even though it was so early in the year, which housewives were inspecting. Paris was very cheerful that morning, with the shady pavements more crowded than those directly in the sunshine.

Turning into Rue Notre-Dame-de-Lorette, they spotted the yellow front of the Saint-Trop'. There was a metal grille across the door and, to the left of it, a frame containing photographs of nude women.

On Rue Victor-Massé, an almost identical frame hung on the longer façade of the Train Bleu. Lucas stopped a little further down the street in front of a smart building. The block was greyish, relatively prosperous-looking, and a couple of brass plates announced the offices of a doctor and an estate agent respectively.

'What is it?' asked an unfriendly concierge, opening her glazed door.

'Madame Boulay . . .'

'Third floor on the left, but . . .'

She studied the two men, then changed her mind:

'Are you from the police? Then you can go up . . . Those poor women must be in an awful state.'

There was an all but silent lift and a red carpet on the stairs, which were better lit than in most of the old buildings in Paris. On the third floor voices could be heard behind a door. Maigret rang the bell, and the voices fell silent. Footsteps came nearer, then Antonio appeared in the doorway. He had taken off his jacket and was holding a sandwich.

'Come in . . . Ignore the mess.'

A baby was crying in a bedroom. A little boy clung to the dress of a young woman, who was already quite fat for her age. She hadn't had time to do her black hair, which spilled over her shoulders.

'My sister Marina . . .'

Her eyes were red, unsurprisingly, and she seemed a little lost.

'Come this way.'

She showed them into a messy living room with an upturned rocking horse on the carpet and some dirty cups and glasses on the table.

An older, much fatter woman dressed in a sky-blue

housecoat appeared in another doorway and studied the newcomers warily.

'My mother,' introduced Antonio. 'She barely speaks French. She'll never get the hang of it.'

The apartment seemed spacious and comfortable, furnished with the sort of rustic furniture you find in the big department stores.

'Where is your sister?' asked Maigret, looking round.

'With the baby . . . She's coming.'

'How do you explain all this, detective chief inspector?' asked Marina, whose accent was weaker than her brother's.

She had been eighteen or nineteen when Boulay met her, which meant she was twenty-five or twenty-six now. She was still very beautiful, with an olive complexion, dark eyes. Were her looks still important to her? It wasn't easy to tell in the circumstances, but Maigret would have bet that she wasn't interested in her figure and make-up any more, that she was happy living with her mother, her sister, her children and her husband and didn't spare a thought for anyone else.

The moment he came in Maigret had sniffed the air, recognizing a rich aroma that reminded him of Italian restaurants.

Antonio had clearly become the head of the family. Hadn't he already been that to some extent when Émile Boulay was alive? The former cruise-ship waiter would have had to ask him for Marina's hand, wouldn't he?

'Have you found out anything?' Antonio asked, still holding his sandwich.

'I'd like to know if he had his automatic on him when he went out on Tuesday evening.'

Antonio looked at his sister, who hesitated for a moment, then hurried into another room. She didn't shut the door, so Maigret saw her walk through a dining room and into a bedroom. She opened a drawer in a chest of drawers, then came back with a dark object in her hand.

It was the automatic. She held it gingerly, as if she was afraid of guns.

'It was in its usual place,' she said.

'Didn't he always have it on him?'

'Not the whole time, no. Not recently.'

'Since Mazotti died and his gang went back down south,' Antonio put in, 'Émile didn't feel he needed to be armed any more.'

That was significant. When he had left his home on Tuesday evening, therefore, Émile Boulay hadn't been expecting a dangerous or awkward encounter.

'What time did he leave here, madame?'

'A few minutes after nine, as usual. We had dinner at eight. Then he went to kiss the children goodnight, as he always did before leaving.'

'Did he seem anxious?'

She tried to think. She had very beautiful eyes, which ordinarily must have been smiling and tender.

'No. I don't think so. You know, Émile wasn't an expressive person. People who didn't know him probably thought he was very reserved.'

Tears welled in her eyes.

'But really he was very kind, very attentive.'

She turned to her mother, who was listening, her hands clasped on her stomach, and said a few words to her in Italian. Her mother nodded vigorously in agreement.

'I know what kind of reputation nightclub owners have. People imagine they're sort of gangsters, and it's true, some are . . .'

She wiped her eyes and looked at her brother as if asking his permission to go on.

'He was timid, if anything . . . Maybe not in business . . . He was surrounded by dozens of women he could have done what he liked with, but rather than treat them as most of his colleagues do, he thought of them as employees. He could be firm with them, but he was respectful too. I know that more than anyone because I worked for him before I became his wife.

'You might find it hard to believe, but he spent weeks hovering around me like a teenager. When he talked to me during the show, he just wanted to ask questions: where was I born, where did my family live, was my mother in Paris, did I have brothers and sisters . . .

'He never laid a finger on me all that time. He never offered me a lift home.'

Antonio nodded, as if to say that he wouldn't have stood for anything else.

'Of course, he was familiar with Italian women,' she went on, 'because there's always two or three working at the Lotus. One evening he asked if he could meet my brother.'

'He did the right thing,' admitted Antonio.

The mother must have understood a little French. She

opened her mouth from time to time as if she was about to join in the conversation, but then couldn't find the right words and ended up remaining silent.

A young girl came in dressed in black, looking fresh-faced with her hair already done. This was Ada, who was barely twenty-two and must have been the spitting image of her sister when she was her age. She studied the visitors curiously before telling Marina, 'She fell asleep eventually . . .'

Then she said to Maigret and Lucas:

'Won't you sit down?'

'I understand you were your brother-in-law's secretary, mademoiselle.'

She had the barest hint of an accent as well, just enough to add another aspect to her charm.

'That's a big word. Émile dealt with all his affairs himself . . . And they're not the sort that require a lot of paperwork.'

'Did he have an office?'

'We call it that, yes . . . Two little rooms on the mezzanine above the Lotus.'

'When would he go there?'

'He'd usually sleep until midday and have lunch with us. Then we'd both go to Place Pigalle around three in the afternoon.'

Maigret studied the two sisters in turn, wondering whether Marina, for instance, might not feel a little jealous of her younger sister. He couldn't see any hint of it in her expression.

As far as he could tell, until three days ago Marina had been happy with her lot in life, content to lead a fairly sleepy existence with her mother and her children in the apartment on Rue Victor-Massé. If her husband had lived, no doubt she would have gone on to have a big family.

Ada was a very different proposition, brighter, sparkier. She continued:

'There'd always be people waiting: performers, musicians, maître d's or barmen from one club or other, not to mention the wine and champagne salesmen . . .'

'What was Émile Boulay working on the day he went missing?'

'Wait . . . It was Tuesday, wasn't it? We went downstairs to audition a Spanish dancer whom he hired. Then he saw someone from an air conditioning company. He was planning to have air conditioning put in in all four clubs. The Lotus in particular had problems with its ventilation.'

Maigret remembered seeing a brochure among the dead man's papers.

'Who dealt with the financial side of the business?'

'What do you mean?'

'Who paid the bills, the staff?'

'The book-keeper, of course.'

'Does he have an office above the Lotus too?'

'A little room looking on to the courtyard, yes . . . He's an old fellow who never stops moaning and it pains him every time he has to pay for anything, as if it's his own money. He's called Raison – Monsieur Raison, as everybody says, because if you don't show him some respect . . .'

'Is he at Place Pigalle now?'

'Bound to be. He's the only one who works mornings, because he has evenings and nights off.'

The mother, who had disappeared for a few minutes, returned with a carafe of Chianti and some glasses.

'I suppose each of the clubs has its own manager?'

Ada shook her head.

'No, it doesn't work like that. Antonio runs the Paris-Strip because it's in a different neighbourhood, with a different clientele. It's got a different style, if you see what I mean. Besides, Antonio is family.

'The other three clubs are almost next door to each other. During the evening performers go from one to another. Émile used to go back and forth too, keeping an eye on everything. Sometimes, around three in the morning, we'll send cases of champagne or bottles of whisky from the Lotus to the Train Bleu, say, or if one of the clubs is full and need extra staff, we'll send someone from another where it was less busy.'

'In other words, Émile Boulay managed the three clubs in Montmartre himself.'

'Pretty much. Although they each had a maître d' who was in charge.'

'Meanwhile Monsieur Raison dealt with the book-keeping and paperwork.'

'That's it, more or less.'

'What about you?'

'I followed my brother-in-law around and took notes. Order this . . . Set up a meeting with this supplier or that contractor . . . Ring a performer who's appearing somewhere else to see if we can hire her . . .'

'Did you follow him around at night too?'

'Only for part of the evening.'

'Until when, generally?'

'Ten or eleven. Setting up around nine is the most time-consuming. Someone's always missing, a waiter or a musician or a dancer . . . Or a delivery of champagne or streamers is late.'

'I'm beginning to get the picture,' Maigret said distractedly. 'Were you with him on Tuesday evening?'

'Yes, like every evening.'

He looked at Marina again and didn't see a trace of jealousy on her face.

'When did you leave your brother-in-law?'

'At ten thirty.'

'Where were you at that point?'

'At the Lotus. It was his headquarters in away. We'd already been to the Train Bleu and the Saint-Trop'.'

'Did you notice anything in particular?'

'Nothing. Except that I thought it was going to rain.'

'Did it?'

'A few drops as I was leaving the Lotus. Mickey offered to lend me an umbrella, but I waited, and five minutes later it had stopped.'

'Did you make a note of Boulay's meetings?'

'I'd remind him of them if he needed. I hardly ever had to because he thought of everything. He was a calm, methodical person who ran his businesses in a very serious, responsible way.'

'Was he meeting anyone that night?'

'Not as far as I know.'

'Would you have?'

'I assume so. I don't want to make myself out to be more

important than I was. He never discussed his business or plans with me, for instance. But he did talk about them in front of me. When he met people, I was almost always there. I don't remember him ever asking me to leave the room.

'He'd say things like: "The Train Bleu's wallpaper needs changing."'

'I'd make a note of it and then I'd remind him the following afternoon.'

'How did he react when he heard Mazotti had been shot?'

'I wasn't there. He must have found out that night, like everyone in Montmartre, because that sort of news travels quickly.'

'What about the following day, when he got up?'

'He asked me to get the papers first thing. I went and bought them on the corner . . .'

'Didn't he read them regularly?'

'He'd have a quick look at a morning paper and an evening one.'

'Did he bet on the races?'

'Never. No horses, no cards; he didn't gamble at all.'

'Did he talk to you about Mazotti's death?'

'He told me he expected to be called in for questioning and asked me to ring the maître d' at the Lotus to see if the police had come by.'

Maigret turned to Lucas, who understood his unspoken question.

'Two inspectors from the ninth went round,' he said.

'Did Boulay seem worried?'

'He was afraid of bad publicity.'

It was Antonio's turn to join in the conversation.

'That was always his big worry. He often told me to mind the reputation of my place . . .'

'"Just because we earn our living from showing naked women doesn't mean we're gangsters," he used to say. "I am a reputable businessman and I want everyone to know that."'

'It's true. I heard him say that too . . . Aren't you drinking, detective chief inspector?'

Despite not feeling like Chianti at eleven thirty in the morning, he took a sip to be polite.

'Did he have friends?'

Ada looked around, as if that was a sufficient answer.

'He didn't need friends. This was his life.'

'Did he speak Italian?'

'Italian, English, a little Spanish . . . He'd learned languages on the cruise ships, then in the United States.'

'Did he talk about his first wife?'

Marina didn't seem remotely embarrassed as her sister answered:

'He went to her grave every year, and her picture is still on the bedroom wall.'

'One other question, Mademoiselle Ada. When he died Boulay had a chequebook in his pocket. Do you know anything about that?'

'Yes. He always had it on him but didn't use it much. Monsieur Raison made the big payments. Émile always had a wad of notes in his pocket too. You have to in this job.'

'Your brother-in-law was called in to the Police Judiciaire on 18 May.'

'I remember.'

'Did you go to Quai des Orfèvres with him?'

'To the door. I waited for him outside on the pavement.'

'Did you take a taxi?'

'He didn't like taxis, or cars in general. We went by Métro.'

'He then received another summons for 23 May.'

'I know. He was worried about that.'

'Again because it might lead to bad publicity?'

'Yes.'

'Right, on 22 May he withdrew quite a sizeable sum, half a million francs, from the bank . . . Did you know that?'

'No.'

'Weren't your responsible for his chequebook?'

She shook her head.

'Didn't he let you see it?'

'It wasn't that. It was his personal chequebook; it never occurred to me to take a look at it. He didn't lock it away; he left it on the chest of drawers in his bedroom.'

'Was he in the habit of withdrawing large sums of money from the bank?'

'I doubt it. There was no need. If he needed money, he'd take it out of the till at the Lotus or one of the clubs and leave a note in its place.'

'Do you have any idea why he took out that money?'

'None.'

'Do you have any way of finding out?'

'I'll try. I'll ask Monsieur Raison. I'll look in the correspondence.'

'I'd appreciate it if you could do that today and give me a call if you find anything.'

When they were out on the landing, Antonio asked in a slightly embarrassed voice:

'What shall we do with the clubs?'

Maigret looked at him uncomprehendingly, so he went on:

'Shall we open them regardless?'

'I don't see any reason to . . . But I suppose it's a matter for your sister to decide, isn't it?'

'If we shut, people are going to wonder.'

The lift arrived, and Maigret and Lucas got in, leaving the Italian to his confusion.

3.

Maigret lit his pipe on the pavement, blinking in the sunshine. He was about to say something to Lucas when a typical little Montmartre scene unfolded in front of them. The Train Bleu was not far away, with its neon sign turned off, its shutters closed. Directly opposite the Boulays' building, a young woman rushed out of a little hotel wearing a black evening dress, with a tulle scarf thrown over her bare shoulders. In the daylight, the roots of her dyed hair were showing, and she hadn't stopped to fix her make-up.

She was tall and slim, like a chorus girl. Hurrying across the road on precariously high heels, she went into a little bar, where she was probably going to have coffee and croissants.

Another person came out of the hotel almost on her heels, a Scandinavian businessman type in his mid to late forties, who glanced left and right, then headed to the corner of the street and hailed a taxi.

Maigret reflexively looked up at the windows on the third floor of the building he had just left, at the apartment where three women had re-created a little Italy with two children at its heart.

'It's eleven fifteen. I want to go and see Monsieur Raison in his office. You could ask around the neighbourhood in the meantime, especially the shops – the butcher's, the cheese shop, you know . . .'

'Where shall I find you, chief?'

'At Chez Jo's?'

That was the bar where Mazotti had been shot. Maigret wasn't following any fixed plan. He didn't have any ideas. He was a bit like a gundog running around, sniffing left and right. And the truth was, he didn't mind being exposed to this Montmartre air for the first time in years.

He turned the corner of Rue Pigalle, stopped at the Lotus' metal gate, looked unsuccessfully for a bell. The door behind the gate was locked. There was another club next door, smaller and shabbier, its front painted an aggressive purple, and beyond that a lingerie boutique, its narrow window filled with gaudy bras and knickers.

On the off-chance he went into a block of flats and found a surly concierge in her lodge.

'The Lotus?' he asked.

'Didn't you see it was shut?'

She studied him suspiciously, possibly sensing a policeman.

'I want to see the book-keeper, Monsieur Raison.'

'The staircase on the left, in the courtyard.'

It was a dark, narrow courtyard crowded with dustbins and overlooked by mainly curtainless windows. A brown door was open a crack, revealing an old, even darker staircase which creaked under Maigret's weight. One of the doors on the mezzanine bore a zinc plate with *The Full Moon* stamped on it in crude letters. That was the name of the club next to Émile's.

On the door opposite a cardboard sign read: *The Lotus*.

Maigret had the disappointing impression of entering a theatre by the stage door. Drab and dusty, almost seedy, the setting hardly conjured up visions of evening gowns and bare flesh, champagne and music.

He knocked, heard nothing, knocked a second time, then finally decided to turn the enamel door handle. He found himself in a narrow corridor, where the paint was flaking off the walls. There was a door at the far end and another to his right. He knocked on the latter and, as he did so, heard a scuffling sound. Whoever was inside kept him waiting for a fair while before saying:

'Come in.'

He was greeted by the sight of sunshine falling through dirty windows, a fat man straightening his tie – his age was hard to determine but, with a few grey hairs combed over his bald head, he must have been getting on – and a young woman in a flowery dress standing around, trying to look casual.

'Monsieur Raison?'

'That's me,' answered the man without looking him in the face.

Maigret had obviously interrupted them.

'Detective Chief Inspector Maigret . . .'

It was stiflingly hot, and there was a heady perfume in the air.

'I've got to be off, Monsieur Jules . . . Don't forget what I asked you.'

He opened a drawer with an embarrassed look and took two or three notes from a worn, bulging wallet, which he handed to the girl. In the twinkling of an eye the money was transferred to her bag and she was gone on her stiletto heels.

'They're all the same,' sighed Monsieur Raison, mopping his face with a handkerchief, possibly in case it still had some lipstick on it. 'They're paid on Saturdays and the minute Wednesday comes around they're here asking for an advance.'

Strange office and strange little fellow! It was hard to believe that they were behind the scenes at a cabaret rather than in a slightly shady den of some sort. There were none of the photographs of performers on the walls you'd expect, just a calendar, some metal filing cabinets, a few shelves crammed with files. The furniture might have come from a flea market, and one of the legs of the chair Monsieur Raison pointed Maigret to was mended with string.

'Have you found him?'

The book-keeper hadn't entirely recovered his composure. His hairy hand shook a little as he lit a cigarette, and Maigret noticed that his fingers were brown from nicotine.

In that office overlooking the courtyard, it was almost impossible to hear any noise from the street, apart from a vague murmur. It was another world. Monsieur Raison was in shirt-sleeves, with large patches of sweat under his arms, and his unshaven face was running with sweat too.

Maigret would have bet money that he wasn't married, didn't have a family and lived alone in a dark apartment in the neighbourhood, where he cooked his meals on a spirit stove.

'Have you found him?' he repeated. 'Is he alive?'

'Dead . . .'

Monsieur Raison let out a sigh and piously lowered his gaze.

'I knew it. What happened to him?'

'He was strangled.'

The book-keeper looked up with a jerk, as surprised as Maigret had been at Quai de la Rapée.

'Does his wife know? What about Antonio?'

'I've just come from Rue Victor-Massé. Antonio has identified the body. I'd like to ask you a few questions.'

'I'll answer them as best I can.'

'Do you know if Émile Boulay had any enemies?'

Monsieur Raison's teeth were yellow. He must have had bad breath.

'That depends what you call enemies . . . Competitors, yes. He was too successful for some people's liking. It's a hard profession, no quarter asked or given.'

'How do you explain the fact that Boulay was able to buy four clubs in a matter of years?'

The book-keeper was starting to feel better and was back on familiar ground now.

'If you want my opinion it's because Monsieur Émile ran them the way he would have run a chain of grocer's, say. He was a serious-minded individual.'

'Meaning he didn't sample the merchandise?' Maigret couldn't help remarking sarcastically.

The book-keeper smarted at the dig.

'If you're thinking of Léa, you've got the wrong end of the stick . . . I could be her father. Almost all the girls come and confide in me, tell me their troubles . . .'

'And ask you for an advance.'

'They always need money.'

'So, if I understand you correctly, Boulay's only relations with them were those of an employer with his employees?'

'Of course. He loved his wife, his family . . . He wasn't a tough guy, he didn't have a car, a place in the country or by the sea. He didn't throw his money around, didn't try to impress anyone. That's rare in this business. He would have been successful whatever he did.'

'So his competitors resented him.'

'Not enough to kill him. And as far as the underworld was concerned, Monsieur Émile had earned people's respect.'

'With his dockers.'

'You mean the Mazotti case? I can assure you he had nothing to do with that man's murder. He refused to pay up, simple as that, and to take the wind out of his sails, he called in a few strapping lads from Le Havre. That did the trick.'

'Where are they now?'

'They went home a couple of weeks ago. The inspector in charge said they could.'

He was referring to Lucas.

'Boulay insisted on doing things by the book. You can ask your colleague in Vice, who's in Montmartre almost every night and is a good judge of people.'

A thought crossed Maigret's mind.

'Is it all right if I make a telephone call?'

He rang the home number of Doctor Morel, whom he had forgotten to ask something that morning.

'I was wondering, doctor: is it possible before you get the results of the tests to tell me roughly how long after his dinner Boulay was killed? What? No, I'm not asking for an exact answer. Within an hour, yes . . . I know that based on the contents of his stomach . . . He ate at eight in the evening. What's that? Between midnight and one in the morning? Thank you.'

One little box ticked off.

'I assume you don't work at night, Monsieur Raison?'

The book-keeper with the lonely air shook his head almost indignantly.

'I never set foot in a club. It's not my job.'

'I imagine your employer kept you informed about his business affairs?'

'In principle, yes.'

'Why in principle?'

'Because he didn't talk to me about forthcoming plans, for instance. When he bought the Paris-Strip to set up his brother-in-law, I only found out the day before he signed the papers. He wasn't much of a talker.'

'Did he say anything about a meeting on Tuesday evening?'

'No, nothing. I'll try to explain how the office has always worked. I'm here mornings and afternoons. In the morning I'm more or less on my own. In the afternoon the boss used to come in with Ada, his secretary.'

'Where's his office?'

'I'll show you.'

It was at the end of the corridor, a room barely larger or more luxurious than the one the two men had left. A typist's desk with a typewriter in one corner. A few filing cabinets. Some photographs of Marina and the two children on the walls. Another photograph of a woman, with blonde hair and melancholy eyes, who Maigret presumed was Boulay's first wife.

'He only called me when he needed me. I just placed the orders and settled the bills.'

'So you saw to all the payments, including the ones in cash?'

'What do you mean?'

Maigret may not have worked in Vice, but he still knew how things worked after dark.

'I imagine some payments were cash in hand, off the books, if only to dodge the taxman.'

'No offence, Monsieur Maigret, but you're wrong there. I know it's what everyone thinks about this business, and it sounds easy. But that was what made Monsieur Boulay different from everyone else, as I've already said, the fact that he insisted on everything being legitimate . . .'

'Did you do his tax returns?'

'Yes and no. I kept his accounts up to date and when the time came I handed them over to his lawyer.'

'Let's suppose that at a certain moment Boulay needed quite a large amount of money, half a million francs . . .'

'That's simple. He would have taken it out of the till at one of the clubs and left a note in its place.'

'Did he ever do that?'

'Not for such large amounts. A hundred thousand . . . Two hundred thousand francs . . .'

'So he had no reason to go and withdraw money from the bank?'

Intrigued by the question, Monsieur Raison took his time answering.

'Wait . . . In the mornings I'm here and there's always plenty of cash in the safe. I don't go and put the previous day's takings in the bank until about midday. In any case, I don't think I ever saw him in the office in the morning because he was always still asleep. In the evenings, as I've told you, he could just take it from the till at the Lotus, the Train Bleu or the Saint-Trop'. Afternoons are another matter. If he'd needed half a million in the middle of the afternoon, he probably would have gone to the bank . . .'

'Which he did on 22 May. Does that date mean anything to you?'

'No, nothing.'

'Do you have any record of a payment being made on that date or the following day?'

They had gone back into Monsieur Raison's office. The book-keeper studied a black clothbound ledger.

'None,' he confirmed.

'Are you sure your boss wasn't having an affair?'

'That's completely farfetched, in my opinion.'

'He wasn't being blackmailed, was he? Can you check the bank statements to see if Boulay cashed any other similar cheques?'

The book-keeper fetched a file from one of the cabinets, ran his pencil down the columns.

'Nothing in April . . . Or March . . . Or February . . . Nothing in January either . . .'

'That'll do . . .'

So Émile Boulay had only gone to the bank and with-drawn money once in the last few months. That cheque was still bothering Maigret. He sensed he was missing something, probably something important, and his thoughts were going round in circles. He came back to a question he had already asked.

'Are you sure your boss didn't pay anyone cash in hand?'

'I can't think who he would have. I know it may be hard to believe, but you can ask Maître Gaillard. Monsieur Émile was almost obsessive about this. He used to say that people in slightly marginal professions are the ones that have to be most above board.

'Don't forget that everyone's suspicious of us, the police are on our backs the whole time, not just Vice, the Fraud Squad as well . . . Oh, that's right, talking of the Fraud Squad, I remember a story. Two years ago at the Saint-Trop' an inspector found some counterfeit whisky in branded bottles.

'It goes without saying that that's common practice in lots of places. Naturally Customs and Excise started pro-ceedings. Monsieur Émile swore it was the first he'd heard of it. His lawyer took it in hand, and they were able to prove that the barman was switching the alcohol for his own profit.

'The boss settled up anyway, but I need hardly tell you that the barman was shown the door.

'Another time I saw him even more furious. He had noticed some suspicious characters among the Train Bleu's customers. When you're used to the clientele you can immediately spot anyone who's there for different reasons, you understand . . .

'The police didn't need to step in on that occasion. Monsieur Émile found out before they did that a musician he had recently hired was dealing drugs, on quite a small scale, actually . . .'

'And then threw him out?'

'That evening.'

'How long ago was this?'

'Before the business with the barman, almost three years ago now.'

'What happened to the musician?'

'He left France a few weeks later and now works in Italy.'

None of this explained the 500,000 francs, let alone the death of Boulay, whose body had been kept heaven knew where for two days and three nights, then left in a deserted street by Père-Lachaise.

'Can you get to the club from these offices?'

'Through here.'

He opened a door, which Maigret had presumed was the door of a cupboard, and had to turn on a light, because it was almost pitch black. Maigret saw a steep spiral staircase.

'Do you want to go down?'

Why not? He followed Monsieur Raison down the stairs, which led to a room where a selection of women's clothes, some shiny with sequins or fake pearls, were hung along the walls. There was a dressing table painted grey and cluttered with jars of cream, make-up, eyeliner. The room had a stale, faintly sickly smell.

This was where the performers swapped their everyday clothes for their professional gear before stepping out into the spotlights, out to where men bought champagne at five or six times the going rate for the privilege of admiring them.

First, though, as Monsieur Raison and Maigret did, they had to go through a sort of kitchen, which lay between the dressing room and the club.

Two or three strokes of sunlight filtered through the shutters. The walls were purple, the floor strewn with streamers and multicoloured cotton balls. There was a lingering smell of champagne and tobacco and a broken glass was still lying in one corner, near the band's instruments in their covers.

'The cleaning ladies only come in the afternoon. They clean at the Train Bleu as well in the morning and then go to Rue Notre-Dame-de-Lorette at five, so that by nine everything is ready for the first customers.'

It was as depressing as a beach resort in winter, with its shuttered holiday houses and casino. Maigret looked around as though the décor would give him an idea, a starting point.

'Can I go straight out on to the street?'

'The key to the gate is upstairs, but if you'd like . . .'

'Don't put yourself out.'

He climbed the stairs again and moments later, after shaking Monsieur Raison's clammy hand, was walking back down the stairs that gave on to the courtyard.

It was a pleasure after that to be bumped into by a boy running along the pavement, to breathe the wholesome smell of a vegetable stall as he walked past.

He was well acquainted with the bar belonging to Jo, whom everyone called Jo the Wrestler. He had known it for at least twenty years, if not more, and it had had no shortage of owners. No doubt its popularity had something to do with its strategic position just round the corner from Pigalle, from Place Blanche and the pavements patrolled tirelessly throughout the night by a crowd of women.

Shut down ten times by the police, local villains had invariably reclaimed the bar as a meeting place, and Mazotti wasn't the first to be killed there.

It was peaceful enough, though, at least at that time of day. It was done up like a traditional Parisian bistro, with its zinc bar, mirrored walls and wall seats; four men were playing belote in a corner, while two plasterers in overalls, their faces flecked with white, were drinking wine at the bar.

Lucas was already there, and, as Maigret came in, the owner, a giant of a man with rolled-up sleeves, called out:

'Here's your boss! What can I get you, Monsieur Maigret?'

He was always sarcastic, even under intense questioning. He had experienced his share of that in his career, not that it had resulted in any convictions.

'A glass of white wine.'

Maigret could tell from Lucas's face that he hadn't found out anything significant. He wasn't too disappointed. The investigation was just starting; they were still dipping their toes in the water, as he put it.

The four card players occasionally gave them sardonic,

rather than anxious looks. Jo's voice had a similarly sardonic note when he asked:

'Found him then?'

'Who?'

'Honestly, detective chief inspector . . . You're forgetting that you're in Montmartre, where news travels fast. Émile's been missing for three days, you're roaming around the neighbourhood . . .'

'What do you know about Émile?'

'Who, me?'

Jo liked clowning around.

'What am I supposed to know? Do you think an upstanding businessman like that is going to patronize my establishment?'

This was met with smiles in the card players' corner, but Maigret took a drag of his pipe and drank his wine without letting himself be put out. Then he said gravely:

'He's been found.'

'In the Seine?'

'Actually, no. It wouldn't be too much of an exaggeration to say that he's been found in the cemetery . . .'

'Did he want to save himself the cost of a funeral? I wouldn't be surprised, knowing him . . . Seriously, though, is Émile dead?'

'Has been for three days.'

This time Jo frowned, as Maigret had done that morning.

'You mean he died three days ago, and they only found him this morning?'

'Lying on the pavement in Rue des Rondeaux.'

'Where's that?'

'Like I said . . . A cul-de-sac running alongside Père-Lachaise.'

The card players pricked up their ears. They were obviously as surprised as the landlord.

'He hadn't been there for three days though, had he?'

'He was put there last night.'

'Well, if you're asking my opinion, I think something's not right about this . . . We're having a pretty hot spell, aren't we? It's not going to be very pleasant having a dead body under your roof in weather like this. Quite apart from the fact that that's a strange place to drop off that sort of parcel. Unless a maniac did it.'

'Come on, Jo, it won't hurt you to be serious for a minute.'

'I'm being deadly serious, Monsieur Maigret!'

'Mazotti was shot as he was leaving here . . .'

'Just my luck! I sometimes wonder if they didn't do it on purpose to get my licence taken away.'

'We didn't give you a hard time, you'll have noticed.'

'Except for the three mornings I was in with your inspector,' rejoined Jo, indicating Lucas.

'I'm not asking if you know who did it.'

'I didn't see anything. I'd gone down to fetch up some bottles from the cellar.'

'I don't care whether that's true or not. I just want to know: in your opinion, could Émile Boulay have done it?'

Jo grew serious. To give himself time to think, he poured himself a glass of wine, filling Maigret's and Lucas' glasses as he did so. He also looked over at the card players' table, as if he wanted to ask their advice or convey the position he was in.

'Why do you ask me that?'

'Because you know more about what goes on in Mont-martre than pretty much anyone.'

'People say that.'

He was flattered all the same.

'Émile was an amateur,' he muttered almost regretfully after a while.

'Didn't you like him?'

'That's another story. I didn't have anything against him personally.'

'What about the others?'

'What others?'

'His competitors. I'm told he was planning to buy more clubs.'

'So?'

Maigret returned to his starting point.

'Would Boulay have been capable of doing away with Mazotti?'

'I told you he was an amateur. The Mazotti business wasn't the work of amateurs, you know that as well as I do. His dockers wouldn't have gone about it that way either.'

'Second question . . .'

'How many are there?'

'This may be the last.'

The plasterers were listening, exchanging winks.

'Go on then! I'll see what I can do.'

'You've just admitted that Émile's success didn't please everybody.'

'Nobody's ever pleased by another person's success.'

'Except that this is a world where everyone plays a tight game, and openings are few and far between.'

'Granted. So?'

'Do you think Émile could have been killed by someone he worked with?'

'I've already answered that.'

'How?'

'Didn't I tell you it's not pleasant having a dead body under your roof for two or three days, particularly in this weather? Let's say the people you're talking about are sensitive souls. Or that they're too closely watched to take risks. How was he killed?'

The story would be in the afternoon papers anyway.

'Strangled.'

'Well, the answer is even more cut and dried then, and you know why. Mazotti was a clean job. If the people from around here had wanted to do away with Émile, they would have done the same. Have you found the people who took care of Mazotti? No, you haven't. And you're not going to, even with your informers. Meanwhile this story of someone being strangled, kept somewhere for three days, then dumped by a cemetery wall, well, that stinks, literally. That's it for your second question . . .'

'Thank you.'

'Don't mention it. Another?'

He held the bottle poised over the glass.

'Not for the moment.'

'Don't tell me you're planning to come back. I've got

nothing against you personally but a little of you goes a long way in this business.'

'How much do I owe you?'

'The second round's on me. When he questioned me for three hours your inspector gave me a sandwich and a beer . . .'

When they were outside Maigret and Lucas didn't say anything for a long time. Eventually Maigret raised his arm to hail a taxi and the inspector had to remind him that they had come in one of the Police Judiciaire's cars. They found it and got in.

'My place,' muttered Maigret.

He had no good reason to have lunch anywhere else. To tell the truth, he still didn't know where to start with this case. Jo the Wrestler, who he knew was being sincere, had merely confirmed what he'd been thinking since that morning.

It was true that Émile Boulay was an amateur who had nonetheless set himself up right in the heart of Montmartre.

And, strangely enough, he seemed to have been killed by another amateur.

'What about you?' he asked Lucas.

Lucas understood the question.

'The local shopkeepers all know the three women. They call them 'the Italians'. They make fun of the old woman and the way she garbles French a bit. They don't know Ada as well because she doesn't go into the shops much, but they used to see her going past with her brother-in-law.

'No one I talked to knew yet. The family seems to be

very partial to their food: it's incredible what they can get through, if the butcher is to be believed, and they always insist on the best cuts. In the afternoon, Marina goes for a walk on Square d'Anvers, pushing the pram with one hand and holding the boy with the other.'

'Don't they have a maid?'

'Only a cleaner who comes in three times a week.'

'Have you got her name and address?'

Lucas blushed.

'I can do by this afternoon.'

'What else do people say?'

'The fishmonger's wife told me, "He's a sly old devil."'

'She was talking about Émile, naturally.'

'"He married the older sister when she was nineteen. When he saw she was starting to put on weight, he sent for the younger one. I bet he'll find another sister or cousin in Italy when it's Ada's turn to fill out . . ."'

Maigret had thought the same. It wouldn't be the first husband he'd seen in love with his sister-in-law.

'Try to find out more about Ada . . . Particularly whether she's got a boyfriend or lover.'

'Is that your impression, chief?'

'No. But we can't leave anything to chance. I'd like to know more about Antonio too. Why don't you take a walk along Rue de Ponthieu this afternoon . . .'

'All right.'

Lucas stopped the car in front of his chief's apartment building. As Maigret looked up, he saw his wife leaning on her elbows at the window. She gave him a discreet wave. He waved back, then set off up the stairs.

4.

When the telephone rang Maigret, who had his mouth full, gestured to his wife to answer it.

'Hello? Who's speaking? Yes, he's eating . . . I'll call him . . .'

He looked at her glumly, frowning.

'It's Lecoin.'

He stood up, still chewing, napkin in hand to wipe his mouth. He had just been thinking about his colleague Lecoin, the head of the Vice Squad, in fact, and had resolved to pay him a visit that afternoon. Maigret's contacts with the Montmartre underworld – Pigalle's in particular – were out of date, and Lecoin knew all the latest developments.

'Hello! Yes, go ahead . . . No, don't mention it. It's fine. I was planning to drop by and see you later.'

The head of Vice, who was Maigret's junior by about ten years, lived not far from Boulevard Richard-Lenoir on Boulevard Voltaire in an apartment that, thanks to his six or seven children, was in a permanent state of uproar.

'I've got someone I'm sure you know here,' he explained. 'He's been one of my informers for a long time. He doesn't like showing his face at headquarters so if he has something to tell me, he comes to see me at home. Today's tip happens to be more up your street than mine. Of course,

I don't know if it amounts to anything, but, apart from his tendency to embellish, because he's a bit of an artist in his own way, he's someone you can trust.'

'Who is it?'

'Louis Boubée, known as Mickey, a nightclub doorman in . . .'

'Send him over.'

'Do you mind if he sees you at home?'

Maigret quickly finished his lunch and, by the time the bell rang, his wife had made coffee, which he took into the living room.

He hadn't seen Mickey, as he was nicknamed, for years, but he recognized him immediately. Not that he could have failed to, really, as Boubée was quite an extraordinary creature. How old must he be now? Maigret tried to work it out. He was still a young inspector when his visitor was starting out as an errand boy in Montmartre.

Boubée hadn't grown a centimetre. He was still the size of a twelve- or thirteen-year-old, and the most extraordinary thing was that he still looked like one too. A skinny little lad, with big, sticking-out ears, a large, pointed nose and a cheeky mouth that looked as if it was made of India rubber.

It was only when you looked closer that you realized that his face was covered in fine lines.

'It's been a while . . .' Mickey exclaimed, looking around, holding his cap in his hand. 'Remember the Tripoli and La Tétoune?'

The two men must have been the same age, give or take a couple of years.

'Those were the days, eh!'

He was referring to a brasserie that used to be on Rue Duperré, a stone's throw from the Lotus. Like its owner, it had had its hour of fame before the war.

La Tétoune was a statuesque woman from Marseilles, reputedly the queen of southern cooking in Paris, who used to greet her customers with a big kiss and call them by their first names.

It was a tradition when you arrived to go and see her in the kitchen, and her clientele would always throw up surprises.

'Do you remember Fat Louis, who owned three brothels in Rue de Provence? And One-Eyed Eugène? And Fine Fernand, who ended up in the movies?'

Maigret knew it was futile to ask Mickey to come to the point. It was a coquettish dance of his: he was willing to pass on information to the police, but only after his own fashion, without appearing to do so.

The men he was talking about were the big underworld bosses of the time, the owners of brothels, which were still in existence, who would meet up at La Tétoune's. They would rub shoulders there with their lawyers, leading barristers for the most part, and actresses, as the place became fashionable, and even government ministers.

'I used to take bets on the boxing in those days.'

Another peculiar thing about Mickey was that he had no eyelashes or eyebrows, which made it strange when he looked at you.

'We hardly ever see you in Montmartre now you're the big chief at the Crime Squad. Monsieur Lecoin passes by from time to time . . . Sometimes I do him a little favour, like I used to with you . . . You know how it is, you hear so many things . . .'

What he failed to say was that he urgently needed the police to turn a blind eye to certain activities of his. As they tipped Mickey when they were leaving the club, the customers of the Lotus had no idea that he had his own thing going on the side.

He'd sometimes whisper into their ears:

'Living statues, monsieur?'

He could say this in a dozen languages, with an explanatory wink. Then he'd slip the address of a nearby apartment into the man's hand.

It wasn't that bad, as a matter of fact. What you were presented with there, dressed up as a great mystery, was a dustier, sleazier version of the show you'd find in almost any club in Pigalle. The only difference being that the women were no longer twenty, but often double that, if not more.

'Your inspector, the little fat one . . .'

'Lucas . . .'

'Yes. He called me in about three weeks ago, after Mazotti died, but I didn't know much.'

He was gradually getting to the point, in his own way.

'I told him that it definitely wasn't my boss's doing, and I was right there. Now I've got a tip-off about who did it. You've always been understanding with me, so I'm giving it to you, for what it's worth, of course. This is not me talking to the police, understand; this is me talking to someone I've known a long time. We're chatting, the conversation happens to get round to Mazotti – who, between you and me, didn't measure up – so, naturally, I say what someone else has told me: don't waste your time looking round Pigalle for the guy who did it. At Easter . . . When was Easter this year?'

'End of March.'

'Right. So, at Easter Mazotti, who was just a little thug trying to make out he was a big man, went to Toulon, and that's where he met the beautiful Yolande. Do you know her? She's Mattei's woman, and Mattei is the head of the gang from Marseille who pulled off a score of hold-ups before they were busted . . . Are you with me?

'So, Mattei is behind bars. Mazotti thinks it's liberty hall and takes Yolande back to Paris . . . Well, I don't need to spell the rest out to you. Mattei still has men in Marseille, so two or three of them go up to Paris to sort it out.'

It was plausible. It explained the Rue de Douai affair, how professional and flawless it had been.

'I thought that would interest you and, not knowing your address, I went to see your colleague . . .'

Mickey wasn't getting ready to go, which meant he either hadn't said his piece or was expecting questions. On cue, Maigret asked innocently:

'Have you heard the news?'

'What news?' Mickey replied, equally innocently.

Then he immediately broke into a roguish smile.

'You mean Monsieur Émile? I heard he'd been found.'

'Were you in Jo's just now?'

'We're not great friends, Jo and me, but the word is out.'

'I'm more interested in what happened to Émile Boulay than the Mazotti affair . . .'

'Well, I've got to say I'm in the dark about that, detective chief inspector. That's the honest truth . . .'

'What did you think of him?'

'Just like I told Monsieur Lucas: what everyone thought of him.'

'What was that?'

'He had his own ideas of how to run his business, but he was above board.'

'Do you remember Tuesday evening?'

'I've got a pretty good memory,' he replied with a smile and one of his compulsive winks, as if everything he said was noteworthy.

'Did anything special happen?'

'Depends what you think's special. Monsieur Émile came by with Mademoiselle Ada as we were setting up, around nine, same as every night. But you know that. Then he went to look in at the Train Bleu and passed by Rue Notre-Dame-de-Lorette.'

'What time did you see him again?'

'Wait. The band had started. So it must have been after ten. We can play all we want to bring in the customers, but they hardly ever show up until the cinemas and theatres have shut.'

'Did his secretary hang around?'

'No. She headed off to the apartment.'

'Did you see her go into their building?'

'I think I watched her go in, because she's a beautiful girl, and I always flirt with her a little, but I couldn't swear to it.'

'What about Boulay?'

'He went back to the Lotus to make a telephone call.'

'How do you know he made a telephone call?'

'Germaine, the coat-check girl, told me. The telephone is just by the cloakroom. The booth has a glass door. He dialled a number that didn't answer and when he came out, he looked annoyed.'

'Why did the coat-check girl notice that?'

'Because usually when he made a telephone call in the evening, he was ringing one of his clubs, or his brother-in-law, and they'd always answer. He tried again a quarter of an hour later.'

'No luck that time either?'

'No. I suppose he was calling someone who wasn't home, and that seemed to irritate him. Between calls, he prowled round the club. He told off a dancer whose dress was the worse for wear and was short with the barman. After a third or fourth go, he came out on to the pavement to get some fresh air.'

'Did he talk to you?'

'He wasn't the talkative sort, you know. He'd just plant himself in front of the door, look at the sky, the cars on the street, then sometimes he'd say if we were going to have a full house or not.'

'Did he get through eventually?'

'At about eleven.'

'Then did he leave?'

'Not immediately. He came back out on to the pavement. He often did that. I saw him take his watch out of his pocket a few times. Finally, after twenty minutes or so, he started off down Rue Pigalle.'

'He was meeting somebody, in other words.'

'I see we have the same idea.'

'Apparently he almost never took taxis.'

'That's true. After his accident, he didn't like cars. He preferred the Métro.'

'Are you sure he set off down Rue Pigalle? Not up?'

'Certain.'

'If he'd had to take the Métro, he would have gone up the street.'

'He did that when he was going to look in at Rue de Berri.'

'So in all probability his appointment was in the neighbourhood.'

'My first thought was that he was going to the Saint-Trop' in Rue Notre-Dame-de-Lorette, but no one saw him there.'

'Do you think he had a mistress?'

'Definitely not.'

With another wink, the wizened urchin added:

'I've got some experience in these matters, you know . . . I'm in the business, in a way, aren't I?'

'Where does Monsieur Raison live?'

The question surprised Mickey.

'The book-keeper? He's lived in the same building for at least thirty years, on Boulevard Rochechouart.'

'Alone?'

'Of course. He's another one who doesn't have a mistress, believe you me. It isn't as if he turns his nose up at women but he wants what he can't afford, so he just bothers the girls when they come into the office to ask him for an advance.'

'Do you know what he does in the evenings?'

'He plays billiards in a café, always the same one, on the corner of Square d'Anvers. There aren't that many billiard rooms left round here. He's practically a champion.'

Another avenue of inquiry that seemed closed. Maigret kept asking questions all the same, not wanting to leave anything up in the air.

'What's his background, this Monsieur Raison?'

'The bank. He was a cashier for I don't know how many years at the branch where the boss had his account, on Rue Blanche. I suppose he gave him a few tips. Monsieur Émile needed someone reliable to do his books, because you can easily get people skimming off in this business. I don't know how much he pays him, but it must be a fair amount because Monsieur Raison left his job at the bank.'

Maigret kept coming back to that Tuesday night. It was becoming an obsession. In his mind's eye, he could see the skinny Monsieur Émile standing under the neon sign of the Lotus, looking at his watch occasionally, then finally striding off down Rue Pigalle.

He hadn't had far to go, otherwise he would have taken the Métro, which was only a hundred metres away. If he had needed a taxi, despite his aversion to cars, there were always plenty driving past his club.

A sort of map was forming in Maigret's mind, the map of a small corner of Paris to which everything kept leading him back. The former cruise-ship waiter's three clubs were close to each other, the only exception being the Paris-Strip run by Antonio.

Boulay and his three Italian women lived on Rue

Victor-Massé. Jo the Wrestler's bar, outside which Mazotti had been shot, was almost visible from the door of the Lotus.

Émile's bank wasn't much further off, and, as a final touch, the book-keeper was a local too.

It was a bit like a village, which Émile Boulay left only reluctantly, if at all.

'Don't you have any idea who he could have been meeting?'

'I swear . . .'

After a silence Mickey admitted:

'I've asked around too, out of curiosity. I like to know what's going on. In my job, you've got to know what's going on, don't you reckon?'

Maigret stood up with a sigh. He couldn't think of any other questions to ask. The doorman had told him various things he didn't know, and might not have known for a long time, but they still didn't explain Boulay's death, let alone the virtually unbelievable fact that someone had kept his body for three nights and two days before dumping it by Père-Lachaise.

'Thank you, Boubée.'

As he was leaving, the little man said:

'Have you come around to boxing?'

'Why?'

'Because I've got a tip for a fight tomorrow if you felt like it.'

'That's all right.'

He didn't give him any money. Mickey didn't sell his favours for money, just the occasional blind eye.

'If I hear anything, I'll call you.'

Three-quarters of an hour later, in his office at the Police Judiciaire, Maigret scribbled something on a sheet of paper, rang the inspectors' office and asked for Lapointe to be sent in.

Lapointe didn't need to look at his chief twice to know where he had got to. Precisely nowhere. He had the heavy, stubborn look he wore in the doldrums of an investigation, when he didn't know how to proceed and was half-heartedly trying every angle.

'Get over to Boulevard Rochechouart and check up on someone called Raison. He's the book-keeper at the Lotus and Émile Boulay's other clubs. Apparently he plays billiards every night at a café on Square d'Anvers. I don't know which one; you'll find it, though. Try to find out as much about him and his habits as you can. I'd especially like to know if he was at the café on Tuesday night and, if so, when he left and when he got home.'

'I'm on my way, chief.'

Lucas was looking into Ada and Antonio in the meantime. To soothe his impatience, Maigret buried himself in his administrative files. By about four thirty he had had enough and, putting on his jacket, went to drink a glass of beer at the Brasserie Dauphine. He nearly ordered a second, not because he was thirsty, but to defy his friend Pardon and his counsels of abstinence.

He hated not understanding. It was beginning to feel like a personal affront. He kept coming back to the same images: Émile Boulay in a blue suit standing outside the Lotus, then going back inside and telephoning without any luck, then kicking his heels, then trying the same number again and again under the coat-check girl's indifferent gaze.

Ada had gone home by this point. Antonio was attending to the first customers of the night in Rue de Berri. The bartenders in all four clubs were straightening their glasses and bottles, the musicians were tuning up, the girls were kitting themselves out in their sordid dressing rooms before they went and took their places in front of the tables.

Boulay had finally got through to the person he wanted to talk to, but he hadn't left immediately. The appointment wasn't immediate, in other words. He had been given a specific time.

He had stood outside the club again, taking his watch out of his pocket several times, then all of a sudden headed off down Rue Pigalle.

He had eaten at eight o'clock. According to the pathologist, he had died four or five hours later, in other words, between midnight and one in the morning.

When he left the Lotus, it was eleven thirty.

He had between half an hour and an hour and a half left to live.

They had established that he hadn't been involved in Mazotti's death. What was left of the Corsican gang knew that as well and had no reason to do away with him.

Similarly, nobody in the underworld would have done the job like Émile's murderer, strangling him, keeping his body for two days and then running the risk of leaving it in Rue Rondeaux.

Ada wasn't aware of her employer meeting anyone. Nor

was Monsieur Raison. Antonio said he didn't know anything. Even Mickey, who had good reasons for being up to speed with everything that went on, was in the dark on that score.

Maigret was glumly pacing up and down his office, pipe stem clamped between his teeth, when Lucas knocked on the door. He was not wearing the triumphant expression of someone who had just made a discovery.

Maigret looked at him in silence.

'I'm hardly any the wiser than I was this morning, chief. Apart from the fact that Antonio didn't leave his club on Tuesday evening, or at any time that night.'

Naturally! That would have been too easy.

'I saw his wife, an Italian woman who is expecting a baby. They live in a pretty apartment on Rue de Ponthieu.'

Maigret's blank stare was making Lucas uneasy.

'I can't help it. Everybody likes them. I spoke to the concierge, the tradesmen, the club's neighbours. Then I went back to Rue Victor-Massé. I found the book-keeper in his office and asked him for addresses of the performers who work at the Lotus and the other clubs. Two of them were still asleep in a boarding house.'

Lucas felt as if he were talking to a brick wall. At times Maigret turned his back on him to watch the Seine flow by.

'Another girl, who lives on Rue Lepic, has a baby and . . .'

Lucas was thrown by how exasperated Maigret seemed.

'I can only tell you what I know . . . They're all jealous of Ada, naturally, although some more than others. They think she would have become the boss's mistress sooner or later, but that it wasn't a done deal yet . . . Antonio wouldn't have approved either, apparently.'

'Is that it?'

Lucas spread his hands disconsolately.

'What shall I do now?'

'Whatever you like.'

Maigret went home early after morosely spending a little longer on the tedious business of the reorganization of police services, which he was sure wouldn't take the form he was recommending anyway.

Reports, always reports! They asked for his advice. They requested he draw up detailed plans. Then it all ground to a halt somewhere in the administrative hierarchy, and nothing more would be heard about it. Unless they decided on the direct opposite of what he suggested.

'I'm going out tonight,' he told his wife in a gruff voice.

She knew it was better not to ask him any questions. He sat down at the table and watched television, grumbling occasionally:

'So stupid!'

Then he went into the bedroom to change his shirt and tie.

'I don't know when I'll be back. I'm off to Montmartre to have a look round a few nightclubs.'

It was as if he was trying to make her jealous. He seemed put out when she said with a smile:

'You should take your umbrella. They're saying on the radio that there's going to be thunderstorms.'

The real reason he was in such a bad mood was that he sensed it was his fault he was confused. He was sure that at some point in the day he had almost been on the right track, he couldn't say exactly when.

Someone had told him something significant. Who, though? He had seen so many people!

It was nine o'clock when he got a taxi, 9.20 when he pulled up outside the Lotus. Mickey greeted him with a knowing wink and held the red velvet door of the club open for him.

The musicians in white dinner-jackets hadn't taken up their positions and were chatting in a corner. The bartender was wiping glasses on the shelves behind the bar. A beautiful red-haired girl in a very low-cut dress was filing her nails in a corner.

Nobody asked him what he was doing there, as if they already knew; instead they just kept darting inquisitive glances in his direction.

The waiters were putting champagne buckets on the tables. Ada, in a dark suit, came out of the back room holding a notebook and a pencil. She saw Maigret, hesitated for a moment, then walked over.

'My brother advised me to open the clubs,' she explained, slightly embarrassed. 'The truth is, none of us knows exactly what we should be doing. Apparently it's not usual to close if there's been a death in the family.'

Looking at the notebook and the pencil, he asked:

'What were you up to?'

'What my brother-in-law always did at this stage of the evening. Checking the stocks of champagne and whisky with the bartenders and maître d's. Then organizing the performers' rota for the clubs. Someone's always missing.

You have to make last-minute changes every night. I also looked in at the Train Bleu . . .'

'How's your sister?'

'She's in a terrible way. Luckily Antonio spent the afternoon with us. The undertakers came by; they're going to bring the body home tomorrow morning. The telephone didn't stop ringing. We had to see to the death notices too.'

She was coping, keeping an eye on preparations as they were talking, as Boulay would have done. She even broke off to say to a young maître d':

'No, Germain. No ice in the buckets yet.'

A new employee, no doubt.

On the off chance, Maigret asked:

'Did he leave a will?'

'We have no idea, and that makes things complicated for us because we don't know what to do exactly.'

'Did he have a notary?'

'Not as far as I know. I'm sure he didn't, actually. I telephoned his lawyer, Maître Jean-Charles Gaillard, but he's not at home. He left early this morning for Poitiers, where he's due in court, and he won't be back until late this evening.'

Who had already mentioned a lawyer? Maigret thought back and lighted on the unappetizing image of Monsieur Raison in his little office on the mezzanine. What had they been talking about? Maigret had asked if any payments were cash in hand to avoid tax.

He remembered the book-keeper replying that Monsieur Émile wasn't the sort of man to cheat and risk getting into trouble, that he insisted on everything being by the book, and that his lawyer dealt with his tax returns.

'Do you think your brother-in-law would have talked to him about his will?'

'He asked his advice about everything. Don't forget that he had no experience of business when he started. When he opened the Train Bleu, some neighbours took him to court, I can't remember why. Probably because the music kept them awake.'

'Where does he live?'

'Maître Gaillard? Rue La Bruyère, in a little town-house roughly in the middle of the street.'

Rue La Bruyère! Barely 500 metres from The Lotus. You just had to go down Rue Pigalle, cross Rue Notre-Dame-de-Lorette and turn left a little further down the hill.

'Did your brother-in-law see him often?'

'Once or twice a month.'

'In the evening?'

'No. Late afternoon. Generally after six when Maître Gaillard was back from the Palais.'

'Did you used to go with him?'

She shook her head.

Strange as it might seem, Maigret's bad-tempered expression had vanished.

'Can I make a telephone call?'

'Would you rather go up to the office or use the booth?'

'The booth.'

Like Émile Boulay, although Boulay had only started trying to call someone at around ten at night. Through the window he saw Germaine, the coat-check girl, who was arranging pink tickets in an old cigar box.

'Hello! Is that Maître Gaillard's house?'

'No, monsieur . . . This is Lecot's Chemist's . . .'

'I'm sorry . . .'

He must have misdialled. He began again, more carefully, heard a distant ring. A minute passed, then two; no one answered.

He redialled the number three times without success. When he came out of the booth, he looked around for Ada and eventually found her in the changing room, where two women were undressing. They paid no attention to him, made no attempt to hide their bare breasts.

'Is Maître Gaillard single?'

'I don't know. I've never heard anything about a wife. But he may have one. I haven't had the opportunity to go to his apartment.'

Moments later, Maigret asked Mickey outside, on the pavement:

'Do you know Jean-Charles Gaillard?'

'The lawyer? I know him by name. He defended Big Lucien three years ago and got him off.'

'He was your boss's lawyer as well.'

'That doesn't surprise me. He's meant to be a hotshot.'

'Do you know if he's married?'

'Sorry, Monsieur Maigret, they're not my speciality, really, those people. With the best will in the world, I can't tell you anything about him.'

Maigret went back into the booth and redialled the number without getting through.

Then, on the off chance, he called a barrister he had known for a long time, Chavanon. He was lucky enough to find him at home.

'Maigret here . . . No, I don't have a client for you in my office. I'm not at Quai des Orfèvres in fact. I'm after some information. Do you know Maître Jean-Charles Gaillard?'

'Not especially. I often run into him at the Palais and I once had lunch with him. But he's too important for a drudge like me.'

'Married?'

'I think so, yes. Wait . . . I'm sure, now . . . He married a singer or a dancer from the Casino de Paris shortly after the war. At least that's what I've heard.'

'Have you met her? Have you been to his home?'

'I haven't been invited.'

'They're not divorced, are they? Do they live together?'

'As far as I know.'

'I don't suppose you know if she goes with him when he has a case out of town?'

'It's hardly usual.'

'Thank you.'

He called Rue La Bruyère again without luck, as the coat-check girl stared at him with increasing curiosity.

Finally he decided to leave the Lotus and, with a quick wave to Mickey, slowly set off down Rue Pigalle. On Rue La Bruyère, it didn't take him long to spot a town-house that on closer inspection proved to be one of those middle-class houses you see everywhere in the country and still occasionally find in some neighbourhoods in Paris.

All the windows were dark. A copper plate bore the

lawyer's name. He pushed the button above it, and a bell rang inside the house.

Nothing moved. He rang twice, three times, as unsuccessfully as when he had telephoned.

Without really knowing why, he crossed the street to get a view of the whole house.

As he raised his head, a curtain moved at an unlit window on the first floor and he could have sworn he saw a face for a moment.

5.

Maigret might have been pretending to be a nightclub owner, doing his best impersonation of Émile Boulay, despite their differences in height and build, as he strolled around the handful of streets that constituted the former Transat employee's universe and watched them change in appearance as the hours went by.

First it was the neon signs that kept flicking on, the uniformed doormen appearing in the doorways. Then it was the jazz spilling out of the clubs, making the air resonate differently, the new faces on the street as the night taxis started to disgorge their fares and a different fauna moved in and out of the shadows.

Women called out to him as he walked along with his hands behind his back. Did Monsieur Émile walk along with his hands behind his back too? He hadn't smoked like Maigret, at any rate. He had sucked mints.

Maigret went down Rue Notre-Dame-de-Lorette to the Saint-Trop'. He had known the club in the past under a different name, when its clientele was mainly ladies in dinner-jackets.

Had Montmartre changed that much since then? The bands played at a different tempo, and there was more neon these days, but the cast of characters looked like the one he used to know. Some of them had simply changed jobs, like the doorman of the Saint-Trop', who greeted Maigret familiarly.

He was a giant of a man with a white beard, a Russian refugee who for years had played the balalaika in another club while singing old ballads from his country in a beautiful bass voice.

'Do you remember last Tuesday evening?'

'I remember every evening God has granted me on this earth,' the former general said grandiloquently.

'Did your boss look in that night?'

'At about nine thirty, with the pretty young lady.'

'You mean Ada? He didn't come back later on his own?'

'I swear by Saint George!' the doorman said, shaking his head.

Why Saint George? Maigret went in, glanced at the bar, the tables bathed in an orange light, occupied by the first customers of the evening. Word of his arrival must have preceded him because the staff, maître d's, musicians and hostesses all gave him curious, slightly nervous looks.

How long did Boulay use to stay? Maigret headed out again with a wave to Mickey, who was outside the Lotus, and another to the coat-check girl, whom he asked for a token.

In the glass booth, he called the Rue La Bruyère number again without any luck.

Then he went into the Train Bleu, which was decorated like a Pullman carriage. The band was playing so loudly that he immediately beat a retreat, plunging into the quiet and darkness of the second half of Rue Victor-Massé, and walked to Square d'Anvers, where only two cafés were open.

One, the Chope d'Anvers, looked like an old-fashioned brasserie in the country. Near the windows, regulars were playing cards, and at the back he could see a billiard table, around which two men were slowly, almost solemnly circling.

One of the two was Monsieur Raison, in his shirt-sleeves. His partner, with a huge belly and a cigar between his teeth, was wearing green braces.

Maigret didn't go in but stood there for a moment, as if fascinated by the show, although he was actually thinking of something else. He started when a voice nearby said:

'Evening, chief.'

It was Lapointe, whom he had given the job of checking up on the book-keeper.

'I was just heading home in fact,' Lapointe explained. 'I've found out what he was up to on Tuesday. He left the café at eleven fifteen – he never stays later than eleven thirty – and less than ten minutes later, he was home.

'His concierge is adamant. She hadn't gone to bed because her husband and daughter were at the cinema that night, and she waited up for them. She saw Monsieur Raison come in and she's sure he didn't go out again.'

The young inspector was puzzled because Maigret didn't seem to be listening to him.

'Have you found anything new?' Lapointe ventured. 'Do you want me to stay with you?'

'No. Get some sleep.'

He preferred to be on his own for his next round of the clubs. It wasn't long before he was back in the Train Bleu, or rather, before he was pulling back the curtain and glancing inside, like those customers who check they've found what they're looking for before they go in.

Then the Lotus again. Another wink from Mickey, who was deep in mysterious conversation with two Americans, presumably promising them unparalleled entertainments.

Maigret didn't need to ask for a token for the telephone. It rang again in the townhouse whose façade he now knew and where he was convinced a curtain had moved.

He started when a man's voice said:

'Yes?'

He had given up expecting anyone to answer.

'Maître Jean-Charles Gaillard?'

'That's me . . . Who's calling?'

'Detective Chief Inspector Maigret of the Police Judiciaire.'

A silence, then the voice said slightly impatiently:

'Well, yes, go on . . .'

'I'm sorry to disturb you at this hour.'

'It's a miracle you got hold of me. I've only just arrived back from Poitiers and I was having a look through my post before going to bed.'

'Could you see me for a few minutes?'

'Are you calling from Quai des Orfèvres?'

'No. I'm a short walk away.'

'I'll be expecting you.'

Mickey was by the door, as always, and the street was getting noisier and noisier. A woman emerged from a corner and put her hand on Maigret's arm, then suddenly drew back when she recognized him.

'No offence,' she stammered.

He walked back to the oasis-like calm of Rue La Bruyère, where a big pastel-blue American car was parked outside the lawyer's house. There was a light over the door. Maigret climbed the three steps, and before he could press the electric button, the door opened on to a white-flagged hall.

Jean-Charles Gaillard was as tall and broad-shouldered as the Russian doorman at the Saint-Trop'. He was a man in his mid-forties with a ruddy complexion and a rugby player's build, who must have been very muscular when he was younger and was only just starting to fill out.

'Come in, detective chief inspector.'

He shut the door, led his visitor to the end of the corridor and showed him into his office. Sizeable and comfortably, but unostentatiously, furnished, the room was lit solely by a lamp with a green shade on a desk partially covered with recently opened letters.

'Sit down, please. I've had a tiring day and the drive home took much longer than usual because I ran into a heavy storm.'

Maigret was fascinated by the lawyer's left hand, which was missing four fingers. Only the thumb was left.

'I'd like to ask you a couple of questions about one of your clients.'

Was the lawyer worried or simply curious? It was hard to say. He had blue eyes and blond, close-cropped hair.

'Of course, as long as client confidentiality isn't at issue,' he murmured with a smile.

He had finally sat down facing Maigret, and his right hand was playing with an ivory paper knife.

'Boulay's body was found this morning.'

'Boulay?' the man repeated, as if he was trying to remember the name.

'The owner of the Lotus and three other clubs.'

'Ah yes, I know.'

'Didn't he visit you recently?'

'It depends what you mean by recently.'

'Tuesday, say.'

'This Tuesday?'

'Yes.'

Jean-Charles Gaillard shook his head.

'If he did, I didn't see him. He may have dropped by while I was at the Palais. I'll have to ask my secretary tomorrow.'

Looking Maigret in the eye, he asked a question in his turn:

'You say that his body has been found . . . The fact that you are here indicates that the police are looking into the matter. Am I to understand that he didn't die from natural causes?'

'He was strangled.'

'Strange . . .'

'Why?'

'Because, despite his profession, he was a good man, really, and I didn't know him to have any enemies . . . It's true that he was only one client among many.'

'When did you last see him?'

'I should be able to give you an exact answer . . . One moment . . .'

He got up, went into the next office, turned on the light, looked in a drawer and came back with a red office diary.

'My secretary keeps a note of all my meetings . . . Hold on . . .'

He leafed through the diary, starting at the back and silently mouthing names. After about twenty pages he exclaimed:

'Here we are! 22 May, at five o'clock. I've found a note of another visit on 18 May, at eleven o'clock in the morning . . .'

'You haven't seen him since 22 May?'

'Not that I remember.'

'He didn't call you?'

'If he called my office, he would have got through to my secretary, so she'll be able to answer that. She'll be here tomorrow at nine o'clock.'

'Did you handle all Boulay's affairs?'

'It depends what you mean by all his affairs.'

He added with a smile:

'That's a dangerous question . . . I'm not sure I'm aware of all his activities.'

'Apparently you filed his income tax returns.'

'I see no harm in answering that. That's right. Boulay wasn't very educated and wouldn't have been able to deal with it himself.'

Another silence, after which he explained:

'I should add that he never asked me to cheat. Of course, like any taxpayer, he tried to pay as little tax as possible, but only by legitimate means. I wouldn't have handled his affairs otherwise.'

'You said he visited you on 18 May. The night before that someone called Mazotti was killed near the Lotus.'

Gaillard lit a cigarette very calmly, held out the silver box to Maigret and then took it back when he saw him smoking his pipe.

'I see no objection to telling you why he came here. Mazotti had tried his protection racket on him and, to get him off his back, Boulay had enlisted the help of three or four strapping fellows from Le Havre, where he was born.'

'I know about that.'

'When he heard about Mazotti's death, he suspected the police would call him in for questioning. He had nothing to hide, but he was afraid of seeing his name in the papers.'

'Did he ask your advice?'

'Exactly. I told him to be completely open. I think, incidentally, that that turned out well for him. If I'm not mistaken, he was called in to Quai des Orfèvres for a second time, on the 22nd or the 23rd, and he came to see me again before that interview. I can't imagine he was a suspect, was he? That would have been a mistake, in my opinion.'

'Are you sure he didn't come back here this week, on Tuesday, say?'

'Not only am I sure, but again the appointment, if appointment there was, would be recorded in the diary. See for yourself.'

He handed the diary to Maigret, who didn't touch it.

'Were you at home on Tuesday night?'

This time the lawyer frowned.

'This is beginning to resemble an interrogation,' he

remarked, 'and I must admit, I'm wondering what's in the back of your mind.'

After a pause, he shrugged and broke into a smile.

'If I think hard enough, I'm sure I'll be able to work out what I was doing. I spend most of my evenings in this study, because it is the only time I can work in peace. Mornings, it's a constant stream of clients. Afternoons, I'm often at the Palais.'

'You didn't have dinner in town, did you?'

'I hardly ever have dinner in town. You see, I'm not a fashionable lawyer.'

'So, on Tuesday night?'

'It's Friday today, isn't it? Saturday, in fact, since it's past midnight. I started out for Poitiers very early this morning.'

'By yourself?'

The question seemed to surprise him.

'By myself, of course, as I was appearing in court there. I didn't leave my office all evening yesterday . . . So what you're really after is an alibi, is it?'

His tone remained light, ironic.

'What intrigues me is that this is an alibi for Tuesday evening, while my client, if I've understood you correctly, has only just died. Anyway! I am like poor Boulay: I want to do everything by the book. On Thursday, I didn't go out. On Wednesday night . . . Let's see, on Wednesday, I worked until ten, and then, as I had a bit of a headache, I went for a walk in the neighbourhood . . . Now, Tuesday . . . I was in court in the afternoon. A tortuous business that has been dragging on for three years and is far from over. Then I went home for dinner.'

'With your wife?'

Gaillard's gaze rested on Maigret and he said very distinctly:

'With my wife, yes.'

'Is she here?'

'She's upstairs.'

'Did she go out tonight?'

'She practically never goes out because of her health. My wife has been ill for several years and is in a great deal of pain . . .'

'I'm sorry.'

'Don't mention it. So, we had dinner . . . Then I came down here, to this study, as usual . . . Ah, right, I've got it . . . I felt tired from my afternoon at the Palais. I took my car, thinking I'd go for a drive for an hour or two to relax, as I sometimes do. I used to play a lot of sport and I miss the fresh air. Driving down the Champs-Elysées, I saw they were showing a Russian film that I had been told was good.'

'To cut a long story short, you went to the cinema . . .'

'Exactly. You see, there's no mystery. Afterwards I went to have a drink at Fouquet's, then came home.'

'No one was waiting for you?'

'No one.'

'You didn't get a phone call?'

He seemed to rack his brains again.

'I can't think of anything, no. I must have smoked a cigarette or two before going to bed, because I have trouble getting to sleep . . . Now really, I have to say, I am quite surprised . . .'

It was Maigret's turn to appear ingenuous.

'Why?'

'I was expecting you to ask me about my client. But all your questions have been about me and what I was doing. I could easily take offence . . .'

'Actually, I am trying to reconstruct Émile Boulay's movements.'

'I don't understand.'

'He wasn't killed last night, but on Tuesday night.'

'But you told me . . .'

'I told you he was found this morning.'

'Which means that since Tuesday, his body . . .'

Maigret nodded. He had an amiable look on his face now and seemed open and confiding.

'It is almost certain that Boulay had an appointment on Tuesday evening. Probably an appointment in this neighbourhood.'

'And you figured he came here?'

Maigret laughed.

'I'm not accusing you of strangling your client.'

'Was he strangled?'

'According to the post-mortem. It would take too long to go through the clues we've collected. He was in the habit of coming and asking you for advice.'

'I wouldn't have seen him at midnight.'

'He might have found himself in an awkward situation. If someone had been blackmailing him, for instance.'

Gaillard lit a fresh cigarette and slowly blew the smoke out in front of him.

'His chequebook shows that he recently took a fairly large sum of money out of the bank.'

'May I ask how much?'

'Half a million francs. That was unusual for him. Normally, if he needed cash he'd take it from the till in one of his clubs.'

'Did it only happen once?'

'Only that one time, as far as we are aware. I'll know for certain tomorrow, when we check his bank account.'

'I still don't see what part I have to play in all this.'

'I'm getting to that . . . Let's suppose he gave in to the blackmailers initially and they came back for more, that they arranged to meet him on Tuesday night. He might have thought of asking your advice. He would have called your number several times during the evening while you were at the cinema. Who answers the telephone in the evening when you're out?'

'No one.'

Maigret looked surprised, so Gaillard explained:

'My wife, as I told you, is ill. She had a nervous break-down initially, which has developed into something more serious. To make matters worse, she suffers from poly-neuritis, which the doctors can't treat. She hardly ever leaves the first floor and always has a maid with her, who is in fact a nurse. Not that my wife knows that. I've discon-nected the phone upstairs.'

'Servants?'

'We have two, who sleep on the second floor. To return to your question, which I understand better now, I don't know of any attempt to blackmail my client. I should also say that I would be surprised if there were such an attempt, because, knowing his affairs as I do, I can't think what he would have been blackmailed about. Which is why he didn't come to ask for my advice on Tuesday night. Which is also why I don't know what he did that night . . .

'When you told me that he had been killed, it didn't come as a great surprise – you don't get to where he was in that world without making some serious enemies. I find it more troubling that he was strangled, and even more so the fact that his body was only found this morning . . . By the way, where did they find it? I suppose it was dragged out of the Seine, was it?'

'It was lying on the pavement by Père-Lachaise cemetery . . .'

'How did his wife react?'

'Do you know her?'

'I've met her once. Boulay was crazy about her. He insisted on me seeing her and the children. He invited me to dinner at Rue Victor-Massé. That's when I met the whole family.'

'Including Antonio?'

'Including the brother-in-law and his wife. It was a real family gathering. Boulay was very petty-bourgeois when it came down to it, and you'd never have suspected from his home life that he made a living from women stripping.'

'Are you familiar with his clubs?'

'I went to the Lotus a couple of times, over a year ago. And I was at the opening of the club on Rue de Berri.'

Maigret was asking himself a lot of questions without venturing to say them out loud. What it meant living with a sick wife, for instance. Did the lawyer look elsewhere for the pleasures he no longer found at home?

'Have you met Ada?'

'The younger sister? Absolutely. She was at the dinner. She's delightful, as pretty as Marina but with a better head on her shoulders.'

'Do you think she was her brother-in-law's mistress?'

'I'm putting myself in your place, detective chief inspector. You have to explore every line of inquiry, I realize that, but even so, some of your theories are mind-boggling. If you'd known Boulay, you wouldn't be asking me that question. He hated complications. An affair with Ada would have turned Antonio against him, and Antonio, like all good Italians, has a strong sense of family . . . Sorry for yawning, but I got up at the crack of dawn to get to Poitiers in time for my trial.'

'Do you usually leave your car outside?'

'I tend not to bother putting it in the garage. There's nearly always space.'

'Forgive me for bothering you like this . . . One last question: did Boulay leave a will?'

'Not to my knowledge. I don't see why he would have either. He has two children. And he married under the convention of common assets. There's no problem with the inheritance at all.'

'Thank you.'

'I'll go and offer my condolences to his widow tomorrow morning and see if there's any way I can help . . . That poor woman!'

There were so many other questions Maigret would have liked to ask him. How had he lost the four fingers on his left hand, for instance. What time had he left Rue

La Bruyère that morning. And because of something Mickey had said, he would also have been very interested to see a list of his clients.

A few minutes later, he was catching a taxi on Place Saint-Georges and on his way home to bed. He got up at eight as usual the following morning and at nine thirty he came out of the commissioner's office, having sat through the daily briefing without saying a word.

His first thought, after opening the window and taking off his jacket, was to call Maître Chavanon, whom he had telephoned the day before.

'It's me again . . . Maigret . . . Am I disturbing you?'

'I have someone in my office.'

'Just a quick question. Do you know any colleagues of yours who are on fairly close terms with Jean-Charles Gaillard?'

'Him again! It's almost as if you bear him a grudge.'

'I don't have anything against him, just a few questions.'

'Why don't you ask him directly? Go and see him.'

'I did.'

'Well, was he difficult?'

'Far from it. The fact remains that some questions are too delicate to come right out and ask someone.'

Chavanon was less than enthusiastic, as Maigret had expected. Professional solidarity applies in almost every field. Members of a particular profession can speak about one another as freely as they want in private, but outside interference is not appreciated, especially not from the police.

'Listen. I've told you all I know. I don't know who he's

friends with these days, but a few years ago he was very friendly with Ramuel.'

'The one who defended the butcher in Rue Caulaincourt?'

'Him, yes. I'd rather you didn't bring me into it if you go and see him. Especially because he's just had two or three acquittals in a row and they've gone to his head . . . Good luck!'

Monsieur Ramuel lived in Rue du Bac. Moments later, Maigret had his secretary on the telephone.

'It's practically impossible. He's busy all morning. Wait . . . If you come around ten to eleven and he gets through his ten-thirty quickly . . .'

The queues at Ramuel's place must have been like at the local dentist's . . . Next!

Maigret went to Rue du Bac anyway, and as he was early, had a glass of white wine at the tobacconist's. The walls of Maître Ramuel's waiting room were covered with signed and dedicated paintings. Three people were ahead of him in the queue, among them an old woman who must have been a rich farmer's wife.

Nonetheless, at 10.55 the secretary opened the office door and discreetly signalled to Maigret to follow her.

Although still young and baby-faced, Maître Ramuel was already bald. He came forward genially with his hand outstretched.

'To what do I owe the honour?'

His office was huge, with wood-panelled walls, Renaissance furniture and genuine Oriental rugs on the floor.

'Have a seat . . . Cigar? Ah no, that's right . . . Please, smoke your pipe.'

Clearly imbued with a keen sense of his own importance, he sat at his desk like an attorney general at the Public Prosecutor's office.

'I can't think of a case I'm working on that . . .'

'It's not about one of your clients. I feel rather embarrassed, actually. I'd like you to consider this a private visit.'

Ramuel was so used to Assize Court trials that he continued to behave in private life as he did in court, with the same exaggerated facial expressions, the same arm movements that could only have been more sweeping if they had been enveloped in the flowing sleeves of a black robe.

He began by opening his eyes comically wide, then spread his hands in a show of surprise.

'Come now, detective chief inspector, you're not going to tell me you're in trouble, are you? Defending Detective Chief Inspector Maigret, what a thing . . .'

'I just need some information about someone.'

'One of my clients?' he asked, assuming an offended air. 'I hardly need remind you . . .'

'Don't worry. I'm not going to ask you to breach client confidentiality. For reasons that will take too long to explain, I need to know something about one of your colleagues . . .'

The lawyer's brows furrowed ostentatiously, as if he was putting on one of his characteristic displays before a jury.

'. . . It doesn't involve betraying a friendship either.'

'Go on. I'm not promising anything, you understand?'

It was annoying, but Maigret had no choice.

'You know Jean-Charles Gaillard rather well, I think.'

A look of mock embarrassment.

'We used to socialize.'

'Did you fall out?'

'Let's say we see one another less frequently nowadays.'

'Do you know his wife?'

'Jeanine? I first met her when she was still dancing at the Casino de Paris. It was just after the war. A delightful girl at the time. And so beautiful! She was known as La Belle Lara. People would turn and look at her as she walked down the street.'

'Was that her name?'

'No. She was actually called Dupin, but her stage name as a dancer was Jeanine de Lara. She probably would have had a brilliant career.'

'Did she give it up for Gaillard?'

'When he married her, he promised he'd never ask her to leave the theatre.'

'Didn't he keep his word?'

This triggered a pantomime of discretion. Ramuel seemed to be weighing the rights and wrongs of answering, sighing heavily as if torn by contradictory feelings.

'Honestly, everyone in Paris society knows anyway! Gaillard came back from the war covered in medals.'

'Was that when he lost four fingers?'

'Yes. He was at Dunkirk. In England, he joined the Free French. He went through the African campaign and then, if I remember correctly, found himself in Syria. He was a lieutenant in the Commandos. He never talks about it, I must say. He's not one of those people who regale you with tales of their wartime exploits. One night when he was meant to be taking an enemy patrol by surprise, the boot was on the other foot, and he only survived by grabbing hold of the knife that was being driven into his chest. He's a tough customer.

'He fell madly in love with Jeanine and decided to marry her. At the time, he was a pupil at Maître Jouane's, the common law specialist, and wasn't earning much.

'Seething with jealousy, he spent his evenings backstage at the Casino de Paris . . .'

'You can guess the rest. Gradually, he got his wife to give up dancing. He started working very hard to provide for her. I often put clients his way.'

'Did he continue practising common law?'

This time Ramuel assumed the embarrassed air of someone wondering if the person he is talking to will be able to understand him.

'It's slightly complicated. There are some lawyers who hardly ever appear at the Palais but nonetheless have substantial practices. They're the ones who make the most money as legal advisers to big companies. They know company law and its every last intricacy inside out.'

'Is Gaillard one of those?'

'To a degree. Mind you, I've hardly seen him for a few years. He's in court relatively infrequently. I'd find it hard to define his clientele exactly. He doesn't represent big banks and industrial concerns, like his former boss . . .'

Maigret listened patiently, trying to guess what he was implying.

'With the current tax laws, many people need expert

advice. Some, given their activities, need to make sure they're on the right side of the law.'

'An owner of a chain of nightclubs, for instance?'

Ramuel feigned surprise, confusion.

'I didn't realize I'd been so specific. Not that I know whom you're referring to.'

Maigret remembered his conversation the previous day with Louis Boubée, alias Mickey. They had both recalled the heyday of the Tivoli and La Tétoune, the mix of underworld bosses, lawyers and politicians you used to meet at her restaurant.

'Boulay's been killed,' he said abruptly.

'Boulay?'

'Monsieur Émile. The owner of the Lotus, the Train Bleu and a couple of other clubs.'

'I haven't had time to read the paper this morning. Was he a client of Gaillard?'

His show of ingenuousness was disarming.

'Obviously that is one of the categories I was referring to. It's not easy avoiding trouble in certain professions. What happened to this Boulay of yours?'

'He was strangled.'

'How horrible!'

'You mentioned Madame Gaillard earlier.'

'Apparently her condition has deteriorated since I lost sight of her. It started back when I was still friendly with them with a series of nervous breakdowns, which became increasingly frequent. I suppose she just couldn't get used to middle-class life. Let's see . . . How old is she now? In her forties, if I'm not mistaken. She must be four or five years younger than him. But she's gone to pieces. She's aged terribly fast.

'I'm not a doctor, detective chief inspector, but I've known quite a few women, great beauties especially, who have taken that change of life pretty hard.

'I've heard that she's almost lost her mind, sometimes spending weeks at a time in a darkened room.

'I feel sorry for Gaillard. He's a clever fellow, one of the cleverest I know, I'd say. He worked very hard to carve out a position for himself. He tried his utmost to give Jeanine a glamorous life, and for a while they lived in very fine style.

'But it wasn't enough. And now . . .'

His expression may have been one of compassion, but there was still a gleeful, ironic glint in his little eyes.

'Is that what you wanted to know? Not that I've told you anything confidential. You could have asked anyone in the corridors of the Palais.'

'I don't suppose Jean-Charles Gaillard has ever had any problems with the Bar Council, has he?'

This time Ramuel flung open his arms, offended.

'Honestly! What do you mean by that?'

Saying which, he stood up and looked at the clock on the mantelpiece.

'I'm sorry but, as you probably saw, I have a number of clients waiting for me. I'm in court at two. I assume no one knows about your visit and that our conversation will remain between ourselves?'

Then, heading towards the door with a buoyant step, he sighed theatrically:

'Poor Jeanine!'

6.

Before going home to have lunch, Maigret had looked in at Quai des Orfèvres and told Lapointe, almost absent-mindedly:

'I'd like you to go and have a look around Rue La Bruyère and the neighbouring streets as soon as you can. Apparently a pale-blue American car is usually parked outside Maître Jean-Charles Gaillard's town-house day and night . . .'

He handed him a piece of paper on which he had scribbled down the car's number plate.

'I'd like to know when the car was there on Tuesday evening, and also when it left yesterday morning or the night before.'

As he said this, he had that look of his: the wide, vacant eyes, the rounded shoulders and lazy, heavy gait.

At such moments people – especially his colleagues – imagined that he was concentrating. Nothing could be further from the truth, but however often he told them, they never believed him. What he was actually doing was a little ridiculous, even babyish. He was taking a glimmer of an idea, the beginnings of a sentence, and repeating it to himself like a schoolboy trying to memorize his homework. Sometimes he would even move his lips or talk in a low voice alone in the middle of his office, or on the street, or wherever he happened to be.

What he was saying didn't necessarily mean anything. Sometimes it sounded like a joke.

'Everyone has heard of the lawyer who was killed by his client, but I've never heard of the client who was killed by his lawyer.'

That didn't mean he was accusing Jean-Charles Gaillard of strangling the puny owner of the Lotus and other clubs. He would have been caught off guard if his wife had suddenly asked him as he was eating, 'What are you thinking?'

He probably would have answered in all honesty that he wasn't thinking anything. There were also the images he was running through his mind as if through a magic lantern.

Émile Boulay, in the evening, standing on the pavement outside the Lotus . . . That was a very common occurrence. The little man liked to go and look at the sky, at the crowd flowing by, changing its rhythm and, as it were, its nature as the evening wore on, and calculate the takings of his four clubs.

The second image was extremely unusual. It was of Boulay going into the telephone booth, as the coat-check girl looked on, and dialling a number that didn't answer.

Three times . . . Four times . . . Between attempts, he went for a little walk around the club or out on the street. It was only on the fifth or sixth attempt that he finally got through.

But he didn't leave immediately. He waited next to Mickey on the pavement, repeatedly taking his watch out of his pocket.

'He didn't go home to get his automatic,' Maigret almost said out loud.

Émile had a licence. He was entitled to carry a gun. When Mazotti and his gang were making trouble for him, he had one on him constantly.

The fact he wasn't armed that night meant that he didn't suspect anything.

And then after a certain time, without saying anything to the doorman, who looked like a wizened little boy, he unhurriedly started walking down Rue Pigalle.

That was the last image. At least the last one of Émile alive.

'Do you have plans for tomorrow?'

He looked up from his plate and stared at his wife as if he was surprised to see her standing there, by the open window.

'Tomorrow?' he repeated in such a blank voice that she burst out laughing.

'You were in a different world! Sorry to . . .'

'What's tomorrow?'

'It's Sunday. Do you think you'll have work?'

He hesitated before answering. He didn't know; he hadn't thought about Sunday. He hated interrupting an investigation, always maintaining that speed was one of the main guarantees of success. The more time elapsed, the harder it was to elicit information from witnesses. He needed to keep up the momentum, to continue exploring the little world into which he had been plunged.

And now along came a Sunday, a break, in other words. And that afternoon was going to be pretty much wasted too because Saturday was almost like Sunday for most people these days.

'I don't know yet. I'll call you this afternoon.'

Spreading his arms out theatrically like Maître Ramuel, he added:

'I'm sorry. There's nothing I can do.'

Naturally the Police Judiciaire was already much sleepier. Offices were empty, detective chief inspectors and inspectors had left for the countryside.

'Isn't Lapointe back?'

'Not yet, chief.'

He had just looked in at the inspectors' office, where the hefty figure of Torrence was showing his colleagues a spinning reel. He couldn't expect everyone to be as mesmerized by Émile Boulay as he was.

He didn't know what else to do on the case while he waited for Lapointe, nor did he have the heart to throw himself back into administrative planning on a Saturday afternoon.

In the end he went in to see Lecoin, his colleague from Vice, who was reading the newspaper. He looked more like a gangster than a policeman.

'Am I disturbing you?'

'No.'

Maigret went to sit on the window-sill, not really knowing why he was there.

'Did you know the owner of the Lotus?'

'I know them all, really.'

Idle and rambling, their conversation went on for nearly an hour without anything coming out of it. As far as

Lecoin was concerned, the former cruise-ship waiter was an honest guy who wasn't part of the underworld, so much so that some people in Montmartre had given him a contemptuous nickname, the Grocer.

By four o'clock it was as if Sunday had come around. Maigret opened the door of the inspectors' office again.

'Lapointe?'

'Not back yet, chief.'

He knew it was pointless, but he still went through the door to the Palais de Justice. That morning he had resolved to go to the clerk's office and get the list of clients Jean-Charles Gaillard had represented in court.

The Palais de Justice was almost empty, its vast corridors echoing and draughty. When he pushed open the door of the clerk's office, he found no one there. It was bizarre. Anyone could have gone in and rummaged through the green filing cabinets that covered the walls from floor to ceiling. Anyone could have gone and taken a robe from the barristers' cloakroom, for that matter, or even sat in the judge's chair.

'The botanical gardens have better security,' he grumbled.

He headed back to his office, and there, finally, was Lapointe.

'I've come back empty-handed, chief. Even though I talked to almost everyone who lives on the street . . . Or at least everyone who hasn't gone away for the weekend.

'They're all familiar with the blue American car. Some know whom it belongs to, others notice it every morning as they're leaving for their work and don't give it another thought. When I asked about Tuesday night, most people rolled their eyes.

'That already seems ages ago to them. Some were in bed by ten, others came back from the cinema at about half past eleven without paying any attention to the cars that are parked all along the road by then.

'The most common answer was: "It's almost always there."

'They're so used to seeing it in its place, you understand, that even if it isn't there, they think it is.'

'I asked around the local garages. There's only one where they remember the car and a big ruddy-faced guy who sometimes comes in to fill it up. But he isn't a regular customer.

'There's still a couple where I haven't been able to question anyone, just because they're closed until Monday morning.'

Maigret opened his arms wide again like Maître Ramuel. What was he supposed to do about that?

'Go back on Monday,' he sighed.

The phone rang. He recognized Antonio's voice and hoped for a moment that he had some news for him.

'Is that you, Monsieur Maigret? I am with the man from the funeral director's. He's suggesting the funeral takes place on Monday at ten. I didn't want to give him an answer without your say-so.'

What concern of Maigret's was that?

'Fine.'

'You'll receive an announcement. The service will be at the church of Notre-Dame-de-Lorette.'

Maigret hung up and stared blankly at Lapointe, who was waiting for instructions.

'You can go. Have a good Sunday. If Lucas is next door, send him in.'

Lucas was there.

'Any news, chief?'

'Not a word. I want you to go to the clerk of the court first thing on Monday morning and get a list of Jean-Charles Gaillard's cases. No need to go back to the year dot. The ones he's handled in the past two or three years will do.'

'Are you going back to Montmartre tonight?'

He shrugged. What was the point? He wished Lucas an enjoyable Sunday, as he had Lapointe, then picked up the telephone.

'Put me through to my apartment . . . Hello! . . . Is that you?'

As if he didn't know she was the only person it could be, as if he didn't recognize her voice!

'Do you remember the times of the Morsang trains? Today, yes . . . Before dinner if possible. Five fifty-two? Would you like to spend tonight and tomorrow there? Good! Pack the small suitcase. No . . . I'll ring myself.'

It was on the banks of the Seine, a few kilometres upstream from Corbeil. There was an inn there, the Vieux-Garçon, where the Maigrets had been spending the occasional Sunday for over twenty years.

Maigret had discovered it during an investigation, a little place tucked away by the river, which was popular with anglers.

Now the couple were regulars. They were almost always given the same room and the same table, at lunch and dinner, under the trees on the terrace.

'Hello! Get me the Vieux-Garçon in Morsang. Near Corbeil . . . The Vieux-Garçon, yes . . . It's a hotel.'

Reading up on it, he had discovered that Balzac and Alexandre Dumas had once been regular visitors, and that later the Goncourt Brothers, Flaubert, Zola, Alphonse Daudet and others had attended literary lunches there.

'Hello! Maigret here . . . What's that? It's beautiful weather, yes.'

This was not news to him.

'Our room is occupied? You have another, but it doesn't look on to the Seine? No matter. We'll be there for dinner.'

So, despite Émile Boulay, they ended up spending a peaceful Sunday by the river. The Vieux-Garçon's clientele had changed over the years. The fishermen Maigret had met in the past had almost all disappeared. They had either died or become too old to get about.

New ones had taken their place, as keen as they had once been. Some prepared their fishing spots days in advance.

You could hear people getting up at four in the morning to go and moor their boats in the current between a couple of stakes.

There was a new, younger clientele as well, mainly couples with little sailing boats who danced on the terrace to gramophone records until one in the morning.

Maigret slept soundly regardless, waking to the crowing of roosters and footsteps of people going off to fish, and finally got up at nine.

Around ten o'clock, as they were finishing their breakfast under the trees, watching the sails manoeuvring on the water, Madame Maigret murmured:

'Aren't you going fishing?'

He didn't have his fishing-rods or tackle, which he had left in their little house in Meung-sur-Loire, but he could always borrow some from the landlady.

Why would a lawyer kill his client? You heard of people killing their doctors because they were convinced they'd been given the wrong treatment, but the opposite was extremely rare. The Bougrat case was the only one he could remember.

Émile Boulay wasn't an aggressive person. He couldn't say his lawyer had failed him because he had never been convicted and didn't have a criminal record.

'Choose any rod you like. The lines are in the cupboard and you'll find some maggots in the usual place . . .'

They walked along the bank in single file and chose a shady spot near a dead tree. As chance would have it, Maigret caught about fifteen roach within half an hour. If he'd had a net, he would probably have also landed the chub weighing over half a kilo which broke his leader.

It is true that he didn't get another bite after that. His wife looked up from her magazine every now and then and watched him with an amused smile.

They had lunch at their usual table while the other guests, as always, turned to stare and whisper. Wasn't the head of the Crime Squad allowed to spend a Sunday in the country like everyone else and fish if he felt like it?

Afterwards he went back down to the riverbank, failed

to catch anything else, and at six o'clock he and his wife were in a packed train heading back to Paris.

They ate some cold cuts and watched it grow dark, looking out at the streets that were still all but empty and the apartment buildings across the way where a few lights were starting to come on.

Boulay didn't spend his Sundays in the country. His nightclubs were open seven days a week, and he wasn't the sort of man to leave them unsupervised. The three women in his life can't have had any desire to leave their Little Italy on Rue Victor-Massé either.

At nine o'clock on Monday morning Maigret stopped off at Quai des Orfèvres to check if there had been any developments, and at 9.45 a taxi dropped him in Rue Pigalle. A funeral notice with a black border was attached to the Lotus' metal gate. There was another on the Train Bleu's door in Rue Victor Massé.

The pavement across the street from Boulay's home was thronged with people. From time to time one of them, or a small group, would break away to go into the building, the door of which was draped in black.

Maigret followed suit, waiting his turn in front of the elevator, where there was a strong smell of flowers and candles. The living room had been transformed into a chapel of rest. Around the coffin stood the dark figures of Monsieur Raison and an old maître d' who was considered part of the family, while a woman could be heard sobbing in a neighbouring room.

Maigret shook hands, then went back downstairs and waited with the others. He recognized faces from the dead man's nightclubs and had the impression that everyone Boulay had employed was in attendance. The women in outlandishly high heels had tired faces, eyes which looked surprised to be seeing the morning sun.

'Quite a turn-out, eh?'

Maigret felt a tug at his sleeve. It was the midget Louis Boubée, alias Mickey. He was dressed in black and seemed proud of the funeral's success.

'They're all here.'

He meant the owners of every nightclub in Paris, including the ones on the Champs-Elysées and in Montparnasse, the musicians, the barmen, the waiters . . .

'Have you seen Jo?'

He pointed to Jo the Wrestler, who waved to Maigret. He was also dressed in black for the occasion.

'There's all sorts here, isn't there?'

Garish suits, showy, light-coloured hats, big signet rings, shoes in suede or crocodile skin . . . Everyone had come out. Boulay might not have been in the underworld, and his nickname, the Grocer, might have been entirely deserved, but that didn't make him any less a part of Montmartre's nightlife.

'Still no idea who did it?'

Just then the lawyer came out of the apartment building, which Maigret hadn't seen him go into, but he was almost immediately hidden from sight by the hearse, which had drawn up alongside the kerb.

There were so many flowers and wreaths that they had to load up two separate cars. The three women got into one car, while Antonio walked behind on his own, followed by several rows of staff and performers. Then came all the other mourners, who formed a cortège over a hundred metres long.

The shopkeepers came out of their shops as they passed, the housewives stopped by the kerb, people leaned out of windows. Meanwhile photographers ran alongside the sombre procession, taking pictures.

The organ resounded as six pallbearers entered the church with the coffin. The women followed, heavily veiled. For a moment, Jean-Charles Gaillard's and Maigret's eyes met, then the two men were separated by the crowd.

Maigret stayed at the back of the church, where a ray of sunshine fell across the floor every time the door opened. He went on shuffling through the same images in his mind, like a pack of cards.

Boulay taking his watch out of his pocket . . . Boulay waiting for a few minutes before going down Rue Pigalle . . .

Antonio had done a good job. The prayers of absolution were accompanied by a sung mass.

It took a long time for everyone to leave the church. Four or five cars were waiting outside to take the family and their closest associates to Ivry, where Boulay was going to be buried, as Montmartre's cemetery was full.

Antonio found time to turn in the crowd and go up to Maigret.

'Shall we save you a seat?'

Maigret shook his head. His eyes were fixed on the lawyer, who was walking away. He elbowed his way over to him.

'A fine funeral,' he said, a bit like Mickey in Rue Victor-Massé. 'Aren't you going to the cemetery?'

'I've got some work to do. Besides, I wasn't invited.'

'All of Montmartre was there.'

The crowd was still dispersing as the hearse and cars drove off.

'You must have spotted quite a few of your clients.'

'That's what it's like being a lawyer.'

Changing the subject, as if he found this one unpleasant, Gaillard asked:

'Do you have a lead?'

'Let's call it the beginnings of a lead.'

'Meaning?'

'I'm still missing the most important thing, the motive.'

'Have you got everything else?'

'No proof yet, unfortunately! Did you go to the country yesterday?'

The lawyer looked at him in surprise.

'Why do you ask?'

Like many other mourners, they were walking back up Rue Notre-Dame-de-Lorette, which can rarely have been so busy at that hour of the morning. They passed the Saint-Trop', where the photographs of naked women had been taken down and replaced with the funeral notice.

'No reason,' replied Maigret. 'Because I went there with my wife. Because most Parisians go to the country or the seaside on a Sunday.'

'My wife hasn't been mobile for a long time.'

'So you spend your Sundays alone in Rue La Bruyère?'

'It's a chance to go over my cases.'

Was Jean-Charles Gaillard wondering why Maigret was dogging his footsteps? Normally Maigret would have headed down towards the centre of town, but he kept walking along in step with the lawyer, and they soon found themselves in Rue La Bruyère, where the blue car was in its usual spot in front of the town-house.

There was an awkward moment. Maigret made no move to leave, as the lawyer stood holding his front-door keys.

'I'm not inviting you in because I know how busy you are.'

'Actually I was just going to ask if I could make a telephone call.'

The door swung open.

'Come into my office.'

The door to the adjoining office was open, and a secretary in her thirties stood up. Without taking any notice of Maigret, she said to her employer,

'There have been two calls, one from Cannes—'

'In a minute, Lucette.'

Gaillard seemed preoccupied.

'Do you want to call a Paris number? The telephone's there, in front of you.'

'Thank you.'

The window looked on to a paved courtyard with a rather beautiful lime tree in the middle.

Maigret stood and dialled a number.

'Hello! Has Inspector Lapointe come back? Put him on, will you . . . Thank you. Yes . . . Hello . . . Lapointe? Did you find what you were looking for?'

He listened for a long time while the lawyer moved around, rearranging files without sitting down at his desk.

'Yes . . . Yes . . . I understand. Are you sure of the dates? Did you get him to sign a statement? No, I'm at Rue La Bruyère. Is Lucas back? Not yet?'

As he talked, he looked at the courtyard and saw a couple of blackbirds hopping about on the paving stones and the lawyer's shadow as he walked back and forth in front of the window.

'Wait for me, yes. I won't be long, and I may have some news.'

He was entitled to put on a little act too, wasn't he? Hanging up the telephone, he pretended to be embarrassed, scratching his head with a puzzled expression.

The two of them were still standing, and the lawyer was looking at him inquisitively. Maigret purposefully let the silence drag on. He broke it finally to say, with a hint of reproach in his voice, 'Your memory isn't very good, Monsieur Gaillard.'

'What are you implying?'

'Or, for some reason I can't work out, you didn't tell me the truth.'

'About what?'

'Don't you know?'

'I swear.'

This tall, strong man had been entirely sure of himself a few moments earlier. Now his face was like a little boy's who has been caught doing something wrong but is still trying to act innocent.

'I really don't know what you mean.'

'May I smoke?'

'Please do.'

Maigret slowly filled his pipe, scowling like a man with an unpleasant task ahead of him.

'Wouldn't you like to sit down?' the lawyer offered.

'I'll only be a moment. When I came to see you on Friday, I spoke to you about your car . . .'

'You may have . . . We had a rather haphazard conversation, and I was sufficiently affected by what I'd just heard not to take in all the details.'

'You told me that your car was usually parked in front of your house and that you left it there overnight.'

'That's correct. It spent last night there, and the night before. You may have seen it when you came in . . .'

'But there were some days recently when it wasn't there.'

The lawyer made as if to rack his brains.

'Wait . . .'

He was very red in the face all of a sudden, and Maigret almost felt sorry him. He was clearly only maintaining a modicum of self-assurance thanks to a huge effort.

'I can't remember if it was last week or the week before that the car needed some repairs. I can ask my secretary. She rang the garage to get them to come and pick it up and fix it.'

There was a silence, during which he made no move for the connecting door.

'Call her in.'

The lawyer pushed the door open eventually.

'Will you come in here for a moment? The detective chief inspector has a question for you.'

'Don't worry, mademoiselle. It's a very innocuous question. I'd like to know what day you called the garage to ask them to come and fetch the car.'

She looked at her employer as if seeking his permission to answer.

'Monday afternoon,' she said finally.

'That's last Monday, is it?'

'Yes.'

She was pretty and likeable, and her white nylon dress revealed an alluring body. Were she and Gaillard . . . ? That was no concern of Maigret's for the moment.

'Did it need a lot of work?'

'I can show you the bill from the garage. It came this morning. They had to put in a new shock absorber. They thought they were going to be able to get the car back on Wednesday morning.'

'But they couldn't?'

'They rang to apologize. It's an American car. They had been hoping the spare parts would be in Paris but they ended up having to call the warehouse in Le Havre.'

Jean-Charles Gaillard was pretending to have no interest in the conversation. He had finally sat down at his desk and was looking through a file.

'When was the car delivered?'

'Thursday or Friday . . . Do you mind? It's in my diary . . .'

She went into her office, then came back instantly.

'Thursday evening. They had the shock absorber sent express and worked on it all day.'

'Did you come back after dinner?'

Another glance at her employer.

'No. I hardly ever do. Only when there's something urgent.'

'That wasn't the case last week?'

She gave an emphatic shake of her head.

'I haven't worked late for at least a fortnight.'

'Thank you, mademoiselle.'

She left the room and shut the door behind her. Maigret remained standing in the middle of the office, his pipe in his mouth.

'Well, there it is,' he grunted finally.

'There what is?'

'Nothing. A minor detail that may be important, or not. You know enough about our profession to understand we can't overlook anything.'

'I don't see what my car . . .'

'If you were in my place, you would . . . Thank you for letting me use your telephone. It's time I was getting back to the office.'

The lawyer stood up.

'Don't you have anything else to ask me?'

'What could that be? I asked you all the questions I wanted to ask you on Friday. I assume you answered truthfully, didn't you?'

'I've no reason . . .'

'Naturally . . . Mind you, the car . . .'

'I admit I forgot about that. It's the third or fourth time

that car has needed work in the last few months, which is why I'm planning to trade it in.'

'Did you get around by taxi for three days?'

'Exactly. I sometimes take taxis even when the car is outside. It saves having to look for a parking place . . .'

'I understand. Are you in court this afternoon?'

'No. I've already told you that I'm not in court very often. I'm more of a legal adviser.'

'So you'll be at home all day, will you?'

'Unless I have a meeting somewhere. Just a moment . . .'

He opened the door of the adjoining office again.

'Lucette! Will you see if I have to go out this afternoon?'

Maigret had the impression the girl had been crying. Her eyes and nose weren't red, but she had a flustered, troubled look.

'I don't think so. All your meetings are here.'

She consulted the red diary all the same.

'No.'

'There's your answer,' concluded the lawyer.

'Thank you.'

'Do you think you'll be needing me?'

'I don't have anything specific in mind, but you never know. Goodbye, mademoiselle.'

She nodded without looking up at him. Jean-Charles Gaillard went out into the corridor ahead of Maigret. The door of a waiting room was half open, and as they walked past Maigret caught sight of the legs of someone, a man, who was waiting.

'Thank you again for letting me make that telephone call.'

'You're welcome.'

'I'll be off now . . .'

When Maigret turned round after walking about fifty metres along the pavement, Gaillard was still on his doorstep, watching him.

7.

It had happened a few times, frequently even, but never in such a clear-cut, characteristic way. He would be pursuing a particular line of inquiry with a doggedness in inverse proportion to how sure of himself he felt or how much actual information he had.

He would tell himself that there was nothing to stop him changing tack at any moment and pursuing a different line of inquiry.

He would send inspectors right and left. He would be convinced he wasn't making any headway, then discover a small new clue and start cautiously edging forward.

And then suddenly, just when he least expected it, the investigation slipped out of his grasp. He wasn't in charge any more. Events took over, forcing him to do things which he hadn't anticipated and for which he wasn't prepared.

In those cases there was always a tough hour or two to get through. He would question himself, wonder if he had been on the wrong track from the start, if it was all leading nowhere or, worse still, to some state of affairs utterly removed from the one he had imagined.

When it came down to it, what had been his only starting point? A simple conviction, backed up by experience, it was true: *Members of the underworld, or mobsters, as they're now called, don't strangle people.* They used guns, or some-times knives, but there wasn't a single strangling in the annals of the Police Judiciaire that could even remotely be ascribed to them.

Another piece of received wisdom was that professional criminals leave their victims where they kill them. Again, there wasn't a single case in the archives of a mobster keeping a body in his home for a number of days before dumping it on a pavement somewhere.

Consequently Maigret had been mesmerized by Émile Boulay's last evening, the telephone calls, him waiting on the pavement beside the uniformed Mickey, the moment when the former Transat waiter had finally strode off down Rue Pigalle.

Maigret's entire hypothesis rested on this and the busi-ness of half a million francs being withdrawn from the bank on 22 May.

It presumed that there weren't romantic rivalries in the Little Italy on Rue Victor-Massé, that the three women got along as well as they seemed to, that Boulay didn't have a mistress somewhere, and finally that Antonio was an honest character.

Only one of these assumptions – or rather, convictions – had to be wrong for the entire investigation to collapse.

Perhaps that was why he still seemed bad-tempered and only proceeded with a sort of distaste.

It was hot that afternoon. The baking sun beat straight in at the window, prompting Maigret to pull down the blind. He and Lucas had taken off their jackets and, behind closed doors, were working on something that would probably have elicited, at best, a shrug from an examining magistrate.

It was true that the magistrate in charge of the case was leaving them in peace, convinced that it was just a trivial settling of criminal scores. The press didn't seem remotely interested either.

'Lawyers don't kill their clients . . .'

This was becoming a refrain that Maigret couldn't get out of his head, like a song he had heard too often on the radio or television.

'Lawyers . . .'

Be that as it may, he had still gone to Maître Jean-Charles Gaillard's house that morning after the funeral, but he had been as circumspect as possible. Falling in with the lawyer as if by accident as they were coming out of the church, he had accompanied him as far as Rue La Bruyère and made sure not to be too insistent in his questioning.

'Lawyers don't kill . . .'

It was no more incontrovertible or well-reasoned than the other assertion he had taken as his initial premise:

'Mobsters don't strangle . . .'

But you didn't call a well-known lawyer into Quai des Orfèvres and subject him to several hours' questioning without risking having the whole bar, if not the whole judiciary, on your back.

Some professions are more sensitive than others. He had noticed this when he had telephoned his friend Chavanon, and again when he had visited the ineffable Maître Ramuel.

'Lawyers don't kill their clients . . .'

And yet Jean-Charles Gaillard's clients were the focus of the two men's attention in the golden light of Maigret's office. Lucas had come back from court with a list that a clerk of the court had helped him compile.

Lucas was also beginning to have an idea. It was still vague. He couldn't exactly articulate what he was thinking.

'The clerk told me something strange . . .'

'What?'

'He gave an odd smile when I mentioned Jean-Charles Gaillard's name, for a start. Then I asked him for a list of cases Gaillard had taken on in the last two years, and he had even more of a mischievous glint in his eye.

'"You won't find many of those," he said.

'"Because he doesn't have many clients?"

'"The opposite. From what I hear, he has a huge practice, and people say that he earns more money than some of the leading barristers who are in the Assizes every week."'

Lucas went on, intrigued:

'I tried to get him to talk, but for a while he just searched through his files in silence. He was writing down names and dates on a sheet of paper and every now and then he'd mutter:

'"Acquitted . . ."

'Then, after a bit:

'"Acquitted again . . ."

'He still had that sly look on his face I found infuriating.

'"Well, well! Convicted . . . Ah, suspended sentence, naturally!"

'This went on for a long time. The list kept growing. Acquittal after acquittal, and, if not suspended, then light sentences . . .

'Finally I said:

'"He must be very good . . ."

'He looked at me as if he was quietly making fun of me and sneered:

'"Particularly at picking his cases . . ."'

This was the remark that intrigued Lucas. Maigret started turning it over in his mind.

Winning a trial was obviously more pleasant than losing it, not only for the defendant but also for his legal representative. The latter's reputation would only grow and his clientele increase with each new success.

Picking his cases . . .

The two men were going through the list Lucas had brought. They had made an initial breakdown. Lucas had written the civil cases on one sheet of paper. As neither of them were familiar with that field, it made more sense to leave it to one side for the moment.

That left relatively few other cases, thirty or so in two years. Hence Jean-Charles Gaillard's claim that he wasn't in court very often.

Lucas went through the names one by one.

'Hippolyte Tessier . . . Forgery . . . Acquitted on 1 September.'

Both racked their brains. If they couldn't remember anything, Maigret went and opened the door of the inspectors' office.

'Tessier . . . Forgery . . . Ring any bells?'

'Wasn't he the manager of a casino somewhere in Brittany who tried to set up an illegal gambling den in Paris?'

They moved on to the next case.

'Julien Vendre . . . Burglary . . . Acquitted.'

Maigret remembered him. He was a quiet man with the looks of a sad little clerk who had specialized in stealing transistors. He hadn't been caught red-handed, and they didn't have any hard evidence against him. Maigret had advised the judge not to press charges but to wait until he got himself in deeper.

'Put him on the third piece of paper.'

As they worked like this, the hefty figure of Torrence was sitting on a shady café terrace opposite the lawyer's house, and an unmarked police car was waiting a few metres down the road, not far from the blue American car.

If Torrence had to sit at his table all afternoon watching the door opposite, how many glasses of beer would he get through?

'Urbain Potier . . . Receiving stolen goods . . . One year in prison, sentence suspended.'

Lucas had handled that case a few months earlier, and the man had come in to Quai des Orfèvres several times, a fat character as dishevelled as Monsieur Raison, the bookkeeper, with tufts of black hair sticking out of his nostrils.

He ran a junk shop on Boulevard de la Chapelle. You could find anything there, from old oil lamps to refrigerators and tatty clothes.

'I'm an honest shopkeeper. Humble, but honest. I had no idea when this guy came in to sell me some lead piping that he'd stolen it. I took him for . . .'

Maigret hesitated at every name. The door of the inspectors' office was opened ten times.

'Add him . . .'

'Gaston Mauran . . . Car theft.'

'A kid with red hair?'

'It doesn't say here.'

'Last spring?'

'Yes. April. There was a gang repainting cars and sending them to dealers in the country.'

'Call Dupeu.'

Inspector Dupeu, who had been in charge of the investigation, happened to be next door.

'Is this the red-haired kid who trotted out the story of his sick old mother?'

'Yes, chief. There actually was a sick old mother. He was only nineteen at the time. He was the junior member of the gang. He just kept lookout while Mad Justin stole the cars . . .'

Two cases of pimping, a few more burglaries. Nothing momentous. Nothing that would have made the front page.

On the other hand, all the lawyer's clients were broadly speaking professionals.

'Go on,' sighed Maigret.

'That's it. You told me not to go back more than two years.'

There wasn't enough in there to take up the time of a lawyer who lived in a Parisian town-house, even if it was a fairly ordinary family home.

Of course you had to allow for the cases of his that hadn't gone to court, which was probably most of them.

And then there was another type of client, like Boulay, who paid Jean-Charles Gaillard to do their tax returns.

Maigret was floundering. He was hot and thirsty and felt himself getting bogged down. He was tempted to start all over again.

'Get the inspector of taxes for the ninth arrondissement on the telephone.'

It seemed like a shot in the dark, but he couldn't justify leaving anything to chance at this point.

'What? Monsieur Jubelin? Well then, get Monsieur Jubelin on the telephone. I'm calling on Detective Chief Inspector Maigret's behalf . . . Police Judiciaire, yes . . . Hello? . . . No, the detective chief inspector wishes to speak to Monsieur Jubelin in person.'

The tax inspector must either have been a busy man or have had an acute sense of his high office, because it took almost five minutes to get him on the telephone.

'Hello! I'll pass you over to the detective chief inspector.'

Maigret grabbed the receiver with a sigh.

'I'm sorry to disturb you, Monsieur Jubelin. I just want to ask you something . . . What's that? Yes, it does concern Émile Boulay indirectly . . . You've read the newspapers . . . I understand . . . No, I'm not interested in his tax returns. That might come up later, but in that case I promise you I'll go through the proper channels . . . Of course, I quite understand your reservations . . .

'I have a slightly different question. Did Boulay have any problems with you? That's it . . . Did you ever have occasion to threaten him with legal proceedings, for example? No. That's what I thought . . . Books always in perfect order . . . Right . . . Right . . .'

He listened, nodding his head and scribbling on his blotter. Monsieur Jubelin had such a ringing voice that Lucas could hear almost everything he said.

'In a word, he had a good advisor . . . A lawyer, I know . . . Jean-Charles Gaillard . . . He's really who I want to talk about . . . I imagine he handled the affairs of a few of your taxpayers . . . What's that? Far too many?'

Maigret winked at Lucas and summoned up his reserves of patience because the tax inspector had suddenly turned voluble.

'Yes . . . Yes . . . Very accomplished, clearly . . . What? Returns that were beyond reproach . . . You tried, did you? And got nowhere . . . I see. May I ask another question? Which social class were Gaillard's clients from, for the most part? A bit of everything, I understand . . . Yes . . . Yes . . . Many were from the same neighbourhood . . . Hoteliers, restaurateurs, nightclub owners . . . Obviously, it's difficult . . .'

This went on for almost another ten minutes, but Maigret only listened distractedly as the tax inspector, after his initial reticence, launched into a minutely detailed account of his fight against tax evaders.

'Whew!' Maigret sighed as he hung up. 'Did you hear all that?'

'Not quite.'

'As I'd expected, Émile Boulay's tax returns were beyond reproach. Our friend Jubelin nostalgically repeated that phrase Lord knows how many times. He's been trying to catch him out for years. Last year, he combed through all his books again without finding the least irregularity.'

'What about the others?'

'Exactly! All Jean-Charles Gaillard's clients are the same.'

Maigret looked absent-mindedly at the list the inspector had drawn up. He remembered the clerk's remark:

'Particularly at picking his cases . . .'

Well, the lawyer was just as good at picking his financial clients: hoteliers in Montmartre and other parts of town who rented rooms out by the hour as well as the night, landlords like Jo the Wrestler, nightclub and racehorse owners . . .

As Jubelin was saying just now on the telephone:

'It's hard proving income and overheads with people like that . . .'

Standing at his desk, Maigret looked through the list again. He had to choose someone, and the rest of the investigation might depend on who.

'Call Dupeu for me.'

The inspector came back into the office.

'Do you know what's happened to Gaston Mauran, who you told us about earlier?'

'A month or two ago, I saw him manning the pumps of a garage on Avenue d'Italie. It was pure chance: I was driving my wife and the kids to the country and wondering where to fill up.'

'Go and ring the owner of the garage and check that Mauran is still working for him. Make sure he doesn't tell him anything. I don't want him getting scared and giving us the slip.'

If it didn't work with him, Maigret would choose another person on the list, then another, and so on until he found what he was looking for.

Admittedly that wasn't very clear. In all the lawyer's cases there was a certain characteristic, some sort of common feature, which he would have had trouble defining.

'*Lawyers don't kill their clients . . .*'

'Do you still need me, boss?'

'Stay here, yes.'

It was as if he were talking to himself and he didn't mind somebody listening in.

'When it came down to it, they all had good reason to be grateful to him. Either they went to court and were acquitted, or the inspector of taxes had no choice but to accept their returns . . . I don't know if you see what I'm getting at. Usually a lawyer is bound to have some dissatisfied clients. If he loses a case, if someone is given a harsh sentence . . .'

'I see, chief.'

'Now, it's not easy picking cases . . .'

Dupeu came back.

'He's still working in the same garage. He's there now.'

'Get a car downstairs from the yard and bring him back here as quick as you can. Don't scare him. Tell him it's a simple check. I don't want him to be too relaxed though.'

It was 4.30, and the heat wasn't letting up, far from it.

There was no air in the room. Maigret's shirt was starting to stick to his back.

'What if we go and have a glass of beer?'

A brief interval at the Brasserie Dauphine while they waited for Gaston Mauran.

As the two men were about to leave the office, the telephone rang. Maigret hesitated before turning back, but ended up answering just to be on the safe side.

'Is that you, chief? Torrence here.'

'I recognize your voice. Well?'

'I'm calling from Avenue de la Grande-Armée.'

'What are you doing there?'

'About twenty minutes ago, Gaillard came out of his house and got in his car. Luckily a traffic jam on the corner of Rue Blanche allowed me to get in mine and catch him up.'

'Did he notice he was being followed?'

'No chance. You'll see why I'm so certain in a moment . . . He headed straight for L'Étoile, taking the most direct route. He couldn't drive fast because of the traffic, and when he got to Avenue de la Grande-Armée he drove even more slowly. We passed garage after garage. It seemed as if he couldn't make up his mind. In the end, he drove into a place called the Garage Moderne, near Porte Maillot.

'I waited outside. I didn't go in until I saw him come out on foot and head off towards the Bois.'

This was precisely the small, unexpected fact that was going to deprive Maigret of his freedom of action, or rather, force him to act at a particular moment, in a way he hadn't anticipated.

His expression became increasingly serious as he listened to Torrence, and he seemed to have forgotten the glass of beer he had promised himself.

'It's a big place with an automatic carwash. I had to show my badge to the foreman. Jean-Charles Gaillard isn't a regular customer; they don't remember seeing him there before. He asked if they could wash his car in under an hour. He's meant to be coming back around five thirty.'

'Have they started working on it?'

'They were about to, but I asked them to wait.'

A decision had to be made immediately.

'What shall I do?'

'Stay there and don't let anyone touch the car. I'll send someone over to bring it back here. Don't worry: he'll have all the paperwork.'

'What about when Gaillard comes back?'

'You'll have an inspector with you. I don't know who yet. I'd rather there were two of you. Be very polite but make sure whatever you do that he comes back here with you.'

He thought of the young car thief he was expecting.

'Don't show him straight into my office. Make him wait. He'll probably be outraged. Don't let yourself be overawed. And, most of all, don't let him make a telephone call.'

Torrence sighed half-heartedly:

'Fine, chief. But get a move on. I'd be surprised if he's going for a long walk round the Bois in this heat.'

Maigret couldn't decide whether to go straight to the examining magistrate to cover his back. But he was almost certain that the magistrate would prevent him acting on his instincts.

In the office next door, he stared at each of the inspectors in turn.

'Vacher.'

'Yes, chief?'

'Have you ever driven an American car?'

'Once or twice.'

'Get yourself over to the Garage Moderne on Avenue de la Grande-Armée as quick as you can. It's at the far end, near Porte Maillot. You'll find Torrence there, who will point a blue car out to you. Bring it back here and leave it in the courtyard. Try to touch as little as possible.'

'Understood.'

'You go along too, Janin, but you'll be staying at the garage with Torrence. I've told him what to do.'

He looked at his watch. Dupeu had only set off for the Avenue d'Italie a quarter of an hour earlier. He turned to Lucas.

'Let's go.'

If they were quick, they could still have their glass of beer.

8.

Before he had the garage mechanic sent in, Maigret asked Dupeu:

'How did it go?'

'He seemed surprised at first and asked me if I worked with you. He was more intrigued than worried, I thought. He asked me twice:

'"Are you sure Detective Chief Inspector Maigret wants to see me?"

'Then he went and washed his hands with white spirit and took off his overalls. Driving here, he only asked one question:

'"Can a case be reopened after it's gone to court?"'

'What did you tell him?'

'That I didn't know, but that I supposed it couldn't be. He seemed confused the rest of the way here.'

'Send him in and then leave us alone.'

As he was shown into the office, Mauran would have been amazed to learn that the famous detective chief inspector was more nervous than he was. Maigret watched him walk into the room, a lanky young man with tousled red hair, porcelain-blue eyes and freckles around his nose.

'The other times,' Mauran began, as if he wanted to come out swinging, 'you left it to your inspectors to question me.'

There was something wily but also naive about him.

'I might as well come straight out and tell you that I haven't done anything . . .'

He wasn't scared. Of course, it made a big impression, finding himself alone with the big chief, but he wasn't scared.

'You're very sure of yourself.'

'Why wouldn't I be? The judge said I was innocent, didn't he? Well, as good as. And I played along, you know that better than anyone.'

'You mean you gave up your accomplices?'

'They'd taken advantage of my gullibility, the lawyer proved that. He explained that I'd had a difficult childhood, that I had to support my mother, that she suffered from ill health.'

Maigret sensed something curious as he was talking. The mechanic expressed himself in a slightly affected way, exaggerating his Parisian salt-of-the-earth accent, but at the same time there was an amused sparkle in his eyes, as if he was pleased with the role he was playing.

'I don't suppose you've brought me in because of that business, have you? I've kept my nose clean since then, I dare anyone to say different . . . Well?'

He sat down without being invited, a rare occurrence in Maigret's office, and even took a packet of Gauloises out of his pocket.

'All right?'

Still observing him, Maigret nodded.

'What if we reopened the investigation for some reason?'

Mauran gave a start, suddenly suspicious.

'You can't.'

'Suppose there are some things I need to clear up?'

The telephone rang on Maigret's desk, and Torrence's voice said:

'He's here.'

'Did he kick up a fuss?'

'Not really. He says he's in a hurry and wants to see you right away.'

'Tell him I'll be with him as soon as I am free.'

Gaston Mauran listened, frowning, as if wondering what sort of act was being put on for his benefit.

'This is a joke, right?' he said after Maigret had hung up.

'What's a joke?'

'Bringing me in here. Trying to frighten me. You know perfectly well that it's all been sorted out.'

'What's been sorted out?'

'Well, you know, that I'm in the clear. No one's going to give me a hard time from now on.'

At that moment he gave a rather clumsy wink, which bothered Maigret more than everything else.

'Listen, Mauran, Inspector Dupeu handled your case . . .'

'The guy who brought me in just now, yes, that's right. I don't remember his name. He was on the level.'

'What do you mean?'

'Well, you know, that he was on the level.'

'But what else?'

'Don't you understand?'

'Do you mean that he didn't set you any traps and went easy on you with his questioning?'

'I suppose he questioned me the way he was meant to question me.'

Implicit in the young man's words, his attitude, there was something ambiguous that Maigret was trying to pin down.

'It had to be like that, didn't it?' asked Mauran.

'Because you were innocent?'

The mechanic seemed to be growing uneasy himself now, as if he no longer understood what was happening, as if Maigret's responses threw him as much as what he was saying threw the policeman.

'Come on . . .' Mauran said hesitantly after taking a drag on his cigarette.

'What?'

'Nothing . . .'

'What were you going to say?'

'I can't remember . . . Why did you call me in?'

'What were you going to say?'

'I think something's wrong here.'

'I don't understand.'

'Are you sure? In that case I'd better keep my mouth shut.'

'It's a bit late for that. What were you going to say?'

Maigret wasn't so much threatening as steely. Standing against the light, he was a solid mass that Gaston Mauran was starting to look at with a sort of panic in his eyes.

'I want to go . . .' he stammered, getting up suddenly.

'Not until you've talked.'

'This is a trap then, is it? Who's messed up? Is there someone around here who isn't in on the game?'

'What game?'

'You tell me what you know first.'

'I ask the questions here. What game?'

'You'll go on asking me that all night if you have to, won't you . . . I was told that but I didn't believe it.'

'What else were you told?'

'That you'd be nice to me.'

'Who said that?'

The boy turned his head away, determined not to talk, but sensing that he would capitulate in the end.

'It's not fair . . .' he muttered finally between his teeth.

'What isn't?'

Mauran suddenly lost his temper. Hackles up, staring Maigret in the face, he shouted:

'You don't know, is that it? What about the hundred thousand then?'

He was so intimidated by the look on Maigret's face that his voice trailed away. He saw the imposing mass coming towards him, two powerful hands reaching out, grabbing him by the shoulders, starting to shake him.

Maigret had never been so pale in all his life. His expressionless face was like a block of stone.

In an unnervingly blank voice, he ordered:

'Say that again!'

'The . . . the . . . You're hurting me . . .'

'Say that again!'

'The hundred thousand . . .'

'What hundred thousand?'

'Let me go. I'll tell you everything.'

Maigret released the mechanic but remained deathly pale. He brought his hand to his chest for a moment and felt his heart beating violently.

'I guess I've been a mug,' Mauran said.

'Gaillard?'

Mauran nodded.

'Did he promise we'd be nice to you?'

'Yes. He didn't say nice. He said you'd be understanding.'

'And that you'd be acquitted?'

'If the worst came to the worst, that I'd get a suspended sentence.'

'Did he charge you a hundred thousand francs to defend you?'

'Not to defend me. It was for something else.'

'To give to someone?'

The young mechanic was so intimidated tears welled in his eyes.

'You . . .'

Maigret stood motionless with his fists clenched for a good two minutes, until finally a little colour slowly returned to his face.

Then he abruptly turned his back on his visitor and, although the blind was lowered, planted himself in front of the window for a while longer.

When he turned round, his expression was almost back to normal, but you could have sworn that he had grown old, that he was suddenly very tired.

He went and sat at his desk, pointed to a chair and unthinkingly started filling a pipe.

'Smoke . . .'

It came out as an order, as if he was exorcizing heaven knew what demons.

In a deadened, muffled voice, he quietly went on:

'I assume you've told me the truth.'

'I swear on my mother's life . . .'

'Who sent you to Jean-Charles Gaillard?'

'An old man who lives on Boulevard de la Chapelle.'

'Don't worry, we're not going to reopen your case. The guy you're talking about is called Potier and runs a junk shop . . .'

'Yes.'

'You'd go out robbing and give him what you'd stolen.'

'It didn't happen often.'

'What did he tell you?'

'To go and see that lawyer.'

'Why him in particular?'

'Because he was in league with the police. I can see now that that's not true. He conned me out of a hundred thousand.'

Maigret thought for a moment.

'Listen. Somebody is going to be shown into this office in a moment. Don't talk to him. Just take a look at him and then go next door with the inspector.'

'I'm sorry, you know . . . They'd made me think it was normal . . .'

Maigret managed a smile.

'Hello, Torrence? Will you bring him in? I've got someone in my office I want you to keep over there in case I need him. Now, yes.'

He smoked, outwardly completely calm, but there was

a sort of lump in his throat. He stared at the door until it opened and saw the lawyer, elegantly dressed in a light-grey suit, quickly take three or four steps into the room, an annoyed look on his face, open his mouth to speak, to protest, then suddenly catch sight of Gaston Mauran.

Torrence couldn't make any sense of this silent scene. Jean-Charles Gaillard had stopped dead. His expression had changed. The young man got up uneasily from his chair and, avoiding eye contact with the newcomer, made for the door.

The two men were left alone, facing one another. Resting both hands flat on his desk, with a great effort Maigret resisted the temptation to get up, march over to his visitor and, despite him being taller and sturdier, slap him about the face.

Instead, in a strangely weak voice he said:

'Sit down.'

He must have been even more intimidating than when he had grabbed the young mechanic by the shoulders because the lawyer obeyed automatically, forgetting to protest against the removal of his car and the fact that two inspectors had brought him to Quai des Orfèvres without a warrant and kept him waiting there like a petty suspect.

'I suppose you've understood the situation,' Maigret began wearily, as if the case was closed as far as he was concerned.

As the lawyer tried to answer, he continued:

'Let me do the talking. I will be as brief as I can because it's hard for me being alone in the same room as you.'

'I don't know what that boy—'

'I told you to be quiet. I haven't brought you in here to question you. I'm not going to ask you for an explanation either. If I had acted on my first instincts, I would have sent you to the cells without seeing you, and you would have waited for the results of the expert assessments there.'

He drew the third list towards him, the list of Gaillard's clients who had gone to trial and either been acquitted or given light sentences.

He read out the names monotonously, as if he was reciting a litany. Then he looked up and added:

'Needless to say, these people will be questioned. Some won't talk, or rather, they'll keep quiet at first. When they find out that the sums they paid for a specific purpose never reached their destination . . .'

Gaillard's face had changed too, but he tried to stand his ground. He started to say, 'I don't know what that young thug—'

Maigret slammed his fist down on the desk, making everything on it jump.

'Shut up!' he yelled. 'Don't you dare open your mouth until I tell you to.'

They had heard the thump from the inspectors' office, and everyone was looking at each other.

'I don't need to tell you how you did it. And I understand now why you picked your clients carefully. Knowing that they would be acquitted, or given a light sentence, it wasn't hard to make them believe that if they paid . . .'

No! He couldn't talk about it any more.

'I have every reason to believe that my name wasn't the

only one you used. You dealt with people's tax returns. I got in touch with Monsieur Jubelin just now and I shall be having a long talk with him.'

His hand was still shaking a little as he lit his pipe.

'The investigation will be a long, complicated one. What I can tell you is that it will be very thorough.'

Gaillard had given up trying to stare him down and lowered his head. His hands were resting on his knees, with a gap where the four fingers of his left hand were missing.

Maigret's gaze fell on that hand and he hesitated slightly.

'When the case goes to the Assizes, your lawyer will bring up your conduct during the war, and probably also your marriage to a woman accustomed to a glamorous life, the illness that has isolated her almost completely from society . . .'

He leaned back in his chair, closed his eyes.

'Mitigating circumstances will be found for you. Why did you need money so badly when your wife was house-bound and you apparently led a solitary life, devoted to work? I've no idea and I'm not asking you either.'

'Other people will ask you these questions, you may understand why. This is the first time, Monsieur Gaillard, that . . .'

He choked up again. He unashamedly got up, went over to the wardrobe and grabbed the bottle of brandy and glass, which were intended for suspects struggling during long, fraught interrogations.

He drained the glass in one, returned to his seat and relit his pipe, which had gone out.

That calmed him down a little, and he spoke in a casual tone of voice now, as if the case no longer concerned him personally.

'Right now experts are going over your car with a fine-tooth comb. I'm not telling you anything you don't know when I say that if it has been used to move a body, there will most likely be traces. That struck you so forcefully that after my visit this morning you felt the need to get it cleaned.

'Don't say anything! For the last time, I'm ordering you to keep your mouth shut otherwise you'll be taken straight to a cell.

'I should also tell you that a team of specialists is on its way to Rue La Bruyère.'

Gaillard gave a start and stammered:

'My wife . . .'

'They're not going there to bother your wife. Looking out of the window this morning, I saw a sort of shed in your courtyard. That will be examined square centimetre by square centimetre. As will the cellar. And the rest of the house, right up to the attic if necessary . . . I'll question your domestic help this evening . . . Be quiet, I said!

'Whoever you choose as a lawyer will have no trouble establishing a lack of premeditation. The fact that your car happened to have broken down leaving you with no means of transport to get rid of the body proves that. You had to wait for the car to be brought back, and it can't have been pleasant spending two days and three nights with a body in the house.'

He had started talking to himself, without even looking

147

at the lawyer. All the little details he had gathered in the past few days came back to him and fell into place. All the questions he had asked himself found an answer.

'Mazotti was shot dead on 17 May and we questioned all the people who had recently been victims of his protection racket. At least one of your clients, Émile Boulay, was called in for preliminary questioning.

'Did he get in touch with you there and then, because you dealt with his financial affairs and had already helped out in a couple of relatively minor matters?

'Either way, he came here on 18 May and was asked the routine questions.

'He was then called in a second time on the 22nd or the 23rd, I don't know why, probably because Inspector Lucas wanted to clear up a few points.

'So, the afternoon of the 22nd was when Boulay took five hundred thousand francs out of his bank. He needed cash immediately. He couldn't wait until the evening to take it out of the till in one of his nightclubs.

'We haven't found any trace of this money . . .

'I'm not asking if he gave it to you. I know he did.'

He said these words with a contempt he had never shown anyone in his life.

'On 8 or 9 June, Boulay received a third summons for Wednesday the 12th. He took fright because he dreaded scandal. Despite his job, or perhaps precisely because of it, respectability meant more than anything else in the world to him . . .

'On the evening of 11 June, the day before he is due at police headquarters, he is feeling both anxious and furious because he has paid five hundred thousand francs to have peace of mind . . .

'At ten in the evening, he starts telephoning your house and gets no answer. He calls back several times, and when he finally gets through, you agree to see him in a quarter or half an hour.

'It's not hard to imagine what he said to you in the privacy of your study. He had paid a lot of money not to get mixed up in the Mazotti affair, not to see his name in the papers.

'But now, rather than leave him in peace as he had every right to expect, the police want to question him again and there's every chance he'll run into journalists and photographers in the corridors of the Police Judiciaire.

'He feels he's been tricked. He's as outraged as Gaston Mauran just now. He tells you that he's going to have a heart-to-heart with the police and remind them of the deal he has struck with them.

'And that's it . . .

'If he left your house alive, if he came here the following morning, gave vent to his resentment . . .

'The rest is none of my concern, Monsieur Gaillard. I have no desire to hear your confession.'

He picked up the telephone.

'Torrence? You can let him go. Don't forget to get his address, the examining magistrate will need him. Then come and get the person here in my office.'

He stood and waited, impatient to be rid of the lawyer's presence.

After a moment Jean-Charles Gaillard, his head bowed, muttered in a barely audible voice:

'Haven't you ever had a passion, Monsieur Maigret?'

He pretended not to have heard.

'I've had two . . .'

Maigret turned his back on the lawyer, determined not to feel sorry for him.

'First my wife, who I tried to make happy in every way I could . . .'

His voice was bitter. There was a silence.

'Then, when she was confined to her room and I felt the need for distraction, despite everything, I discovered gambling . . .'

They heard footsteps in the corridor. There was a quiet tapping on the door.

'Come in!'

Torrence remained standing in the doorway.

'Take him to the back office until I'm done at the Palais.'

He didn't watch Gaillard leave the room. Picking up the telephone, he called the examining magistrate and asked if he could see him right away.

Moments later, he went through the little glass door that separates the police's domain from that of the judiciary.

He was gone from the Police Judiciaire for an hour. When he came back, he was holding an official document. He opened the door of the inspectors' office and found Lucas impatiently waiting for news.

Without any explanation, he gave him Jean-Charles Gaillard's arrest warrant.

'He's in the back office, with Torrence. Drive them both to the cells.'

'Shall we handcuff him?'

That was the regulation procedure, but there were some exceptions. Maigret didn't want to seem to be taking revenge. The lawyer's last words were starting to trouble him.

'No.'

'What should I say to the guard? Should they take away his tie, his belt, his laces?'

More regulations, more special cases!

Maigret hesitated, shook his head and then was left alone in his office.

When he got home a little late for dinner that evening, Madame Maigret noticed that his eyes were glistening and slightly staring, and that his breath smelled of alcohol.

He hardly opened his mouth during the meal. At one point he got up to turn off the television, which was annoying him.

'Are you going out?'

'No.'

'Is your case over?'

He didn't answer.

He had a restless night, woke up feeling irritable and decided to walk to Quai des Orfèvres, as he sometimes did.

He had barely entered his office before the inspectors' door opened. Lucas closed it behind him with a grave, mysterious expression.

'I've got something to tell you, chief . . .'

Did he guess what the inspector was going to say? Lucas often asked himself that question and never knew the answer.

'Jean-Charles Gaillard has hanged himself in his cell.'

Maigret didn't flinch, didn't say a word, just stood there looking at the open window, the rustling leaves on the trees, the boats gliding over the Seine, the pedestrians swarming like ants across Pont Saint-Michel.

'I don't have any details yet. Do you think that—'

'Do I think what?' Maigret asked, suddenly aggressive.

Lucas backed out of the room, stammering:

'I was just wondering . . .'

He slammed the door, and Maigret didn't reappear until an hour later, seemingly relaxed and busy with routine matters.

OTHER TITLES IN THE SERIES

MAIGRET AND THE TRAMP
GEORGES SIMENON

'Maigret was devoting as much of his time to this case as he would to a drama keeping the whole of France agog. He seemed to be making it a personal matter, and from the way he had just announced his encounter with Keller, it was almost as if he was talking about someone he and his wife had been anxious to meet for a long time.'

When a Paris tramp known as 'Doc' is pulled from the Seine after being badly beaten, Maigret must delve into the past to discover who wanted to kill this mysterious figure.

Translated by Howard Curtis

INSPECTOR MAIGRET

OTHER TITLES IN THE SERIES

And more to follow